NIGHT
TRAIN

NIGHT TRAIN

A NOVEL

BY

MARTIN AMIS

HARMONY BOOKS   NEW YORK

Published by Harmony Books, a division of Crown Publishers, Inc., 201 East 50th Street, New York, New York 10022. Member of the Crown Publishing Group.

Random House, Inc. New York, Toronto, London, Sydney, Auckland http://www.randomhouse.com/

HARMONY and colophon are trademarks of Crown Publishers, Inc.

Originally published in Great Britain by Jonathan Cape Ltd. in 1997.

Printed in the United States of America

Design by June Bennett-Tantillo

Library of Congress Cataloging-in-Publication Data
Amis, Martin.
Night train / by Martin Amis.—1st ed.
p.   cm.
I. Title.
PR6051.M5N5   1998
823'.914—dc21   97-28163
CIP
ISBN 0-609-60128-8

10   9   8   7   6   5   4   3   2   1

First American Edition

to Saul and Janis

CONTENTS

PART ONE

BLOWBACK

I am a police. That may sound like an unusual state-ment—or an unusual construction. But it's a parlance we have. Among ourselves, we would never say I am a policeman or I am a policewoman or I am a police offi-cer. We would just say I am a police. I am a police. I am a police and my name is Detective Mike Hoolihan. And I am a woman, also.

What I am setting out here is an account of the worst case I have ever handled. The worst case—for me, that is. When you're a police, "worst" is an elastic concept. You can't really get a fix on "worst." The boundaries are pushed out every other day. "Worst?" we'll ask. "There's no such thing as *worst*." But for Detective Mike Hoolihan this was the worst case.

Downtown, at CID, with its three thousand sworn, there are many departments and subdepartments, sec-tions and units, whose names are always changing: Organized Crime, Major Crimes, Crimes Against Per-sons, Sex Offenses, Auto Theft, Check and Fraud, Spe-cial Investigations, Asset Forfeiture, Intelligence, Narcotics, Kidnapping, Burglary, Robbery—and Homicide. There is a glass door marked Vice. There is no glass door marked Sin. The city is the offense. We are the defense. That's the general idea.

Here is my personal "ten-card." At the age of eighteen I enrolled for a master's in Criminal Justice at Pete Brown. But what I really wanted was the streets. And I couldn't wait. I took tests for state trooper, for border patrol, and even for state corrections officer. I passed them all. I also took the police test, and I passed that, too. I quit Pete and enrolled at the Academy.

I started out as a beat cop in the Southern. I was part of the Neighborhood Stabilization Unit in the Forty-Four. We walked foot patrol and did radio runs. Then for five years I was in the Senior Citizens Robbery Unit. Going proactive—decoy and entrapment— was my ticket to plainclothes. Later, another test, and downtown, with my shield. I'm now in Asset Forfeiture, but for eight years I was in Homicide. I worked murders. I was a murder police.

A few words about my appearance. The physique I inherited from my mother. Way ahead of her time, she had the look now associated with highly politicized feminists. Ma could have played the male villain in a postnuclear road movie. I copped her voice, too: It has been further deepened by three decades of nicotine abuse. My features I inherited from my father. They are rural rather than urban—flat, undecided. The hair is dyed blonde. I was born and raised in this city, out in Moon Park. But all that went to pieces, when I was ten, and thereafter I was raised by the state. I don't know where my parents are. I'm five-ten and I go 180.

Some say you can't top the adrenaline (and the dirty cash) of Narcotics, and all agree that Kidnapping is a million laughs (if murder in America is largely black on black, then kidnapping is largely gang on gang), and Sex Offenses has its followers, and Vice has its votaries, and Intelligence means what it says (Intelligence runs deep, and brings in the deep-sea malefactors), but everyone is quietly aware that Homicide is the daddy. Homicide is the Show.

In this second-echelon American city, mildly famed for its Jap-financed Babel Tower, its harbors and marinas, its university, its futuristically enlightened corporations (computer software, aerospace, pharmaceuticals), its high unemployment, and its catastrophic inner-city taxpayer flight, a homicide police works maybe a dozen murders per year. Sometimes you're a primary investigator on the case, sometimes a secondary. I worked one hundred murders. My clearance rate was just above average. I could read a crime scene, and, more than once, I was described as an "exceptional interrogator." My paperwork was outstanding. When I came to CID from the Southern everybody expected my reports to be district quality. But they were downtown quality, right from the start. And I sought to improve still further and gave it a hundred percent. One time I did a very, very competent job, collating two rival accounts of a hot-potato homicide in the Seventy-Three: One witness/suspect versus another witness/suspect. "Compared to what *you* guys give me to read," pronounced Detective Sergeant Henrik Overmars, brandishing my report at the whole squad, "this is fucking oratory. It's goddamn Cicero versus Robespierre." I did the work as best I could until I entered my own end-zone and couldn't do it anymore. In my time, I have come in on the aftermath of maybe a thousand suspicious deaths, most of which turned out to be suicides or accidentals or plain unattendeds. So I've seen them all: Jumpers, stumpers, dumpers, dunkers, bleeders, floaters, poppers, bursters. I have seen the bodies of bludgeoned one-year-olds. I have seen the bodies of gang-raped nonagenarians. I have seen bodies left dead so long that your only shot at a t.o.d. is to weigh the maggots. But of all the bodies I have ever seen, none has stayed with me, in my gut, like the body of Jennifer Rockwell.

I say all this because I am part of the story I am going to tell, and I feel the need to give some idea of where I'm coming from.

As of today—April second—I consider the case "Solved." It's closed. It's made. It's *down*. But yet the solution only points toward further complexity. I have taken a good firm knot and reduced it to a mess of loose ends. This evening I meet with Paulie No. I will ask him two questions. He will give me two answers. And then it's a wrap. This case is the worst case. I wonder: Is it just me? But I know I'm right. It's all true. It's the case. It's the case. Paulie No, as we say, is a state cutter. He cuts for the state. He dissects people's bodies and tells you how come they died.

Allow me to apologize in advance for the bad language, the diseased sarcasm, and the bigotry. All police are racist. It's part of our job. New York police hate Puerto Ricans, Miami police hate Cubans, Houston police hate Mexicans, San Diego police hate Native Americans, and Portland police hate *Eskimos*. Here we hate pretty well everybody who's non-Irish. Or nonpolice. Anyone can become a police—Jews, blacks, Asians, women—and once you're there you're a member of a race called police, which is obliged to hate every other race.

These papers and transcripts were put together piecemeal over a period of four weeks. I apologize also for any inconsistencies in the tenses (hard to avoid, when writing about the recently dead) and for the informalities in the dialogue presentation. And I guess I apologize for the outcome. I'm sorry. I'm sorry, I'm sorry.

For me the thing began on the night of March fourth and then evolved day by day and that's how I'm going to tell this part of it.

March 4

That evening I was alone. My guy Tobe was out of town, attending some kind of computer convention. I hadn't even started on dinner: I was sitting there with my Discuss Group biography open on the couch, next to the ashtray. It was 20:15. I remember the time because I had just been startled out of a nod by the night train, which came through early, as it always does on Sundays. The night train, which shakes the floor I walk on. And keeps my rent way down.

The phone rang. It was Johnny Mac, a.k.a. Detective Sergeant John Macatitch. My colleague in Homicide, who has since made squad supervisor. A great guy and a hell of a detective.

"Mike?" he said. "I'm going to have to call in a big one."

And I said, Well, let's hear it.

"This is a bad one, Mike. I want you to ride a note for me."

Note meant n.o.d.—notification of death. In other words, he wanted me to go tell somebody that somebody close had died. That somebody they loved had died: This was already clear, from his voice. And died suddenly. And violently. I considered. I could have said, "I don't do that anymore" (though Asset Forfeiture, in fact, is hardly corpse-free). And then we might have had one of those bullshit TV conversations, with him saying *You got to help me out* and *Mike, I'm begging you,* and me saying *Forget it* and *No way* and *Dream on, pal,* until everyone is bored blind and I finally come across. I mean, why say no when you have to say yes? For things to proceed. So I just said, again: Well, let's hear it.

"Colonel Tom's daughter killed herself tonight."

"Jennifer?" And it just came out. I said: "You're fucking me."

"I wish I was fucking you, Mike. Really. This is as bad as it gets."

"How?"

".22 in the mouth."

I waited.

"Mike, I want you to go notify Colonel Tom. And Miriam. This hour."

I lit another cigarette. I don't drink anymore but man do I smoke. I said, "I've known Jennifer Rockwell since she was eight years old."

"Yeah, Mike. You see? If not you, who?"

"Okay. But you're going to have to take me by the scene."

In the bathroom I applied makeup. Like someone doing a chore. Wiping down a counter. With my mouth meanly clenched. I used to be something, I guess, but now I'm just another big blonde old broad.

Without thinking about it I found I had brought along my notebook, my flashlight, my rubber gloves, and my .38 snub.

In police work you soon get to be familiar with what we call the "yeah, right" suicide. Where you go in the door, see the body, look around the room, and say, "Yeah, right." This was definitely not a yeah-right suicide. I have known Jennifer Rockwell since she was eight years old. She was a favorite of mine. But she was also a favorite of everybody else's. And I watched her grow into a kind of embarrassment of perfection.

Brilliant, beautiful. Yeah, I'm thinking: To-die-for brilliant. Drop-dead beautiful. And not intimidating—or
only as intimidating as the brilliant-beautiful can't
help being, no matter how accessible they seem. She
had it all and she had it all, and then she had some
more. Her dad's a cop. Her considerably older brothers are cops—both with Chicago PD, Area Six. Jennifer
was not a cop. She was an astrophysicist, here at
Mount Lee. Guys? She combed them out of her hair,
and played the field at CSU. But for the last—Christ, I
don't know—seven or eight years, it must be, she was
shacked up with another bigbrain and dreamboat:
Trader. Professor Trader Faulkner. This was definitely
not a yeah-right suicide. This was a no-wrong suicide.

Johnny Mac and myself pulled up in the
unmarked. Whitman Avenue. Detached and semide-
tached residences on a wide tree-lined street: An academic dormitory on the edge of the Twenty-Seven. I
climbed out in my stretch pants and my low pumps.

So the radio cars and the beat cops were there,
and the science crew and the medical examiners were
there, and Tony Silvera and Oltan O'Boye were there—
inside. And some neighbors. But them you look right
through. These uniformed figures were churning
under the dome lights. And I knew they swayed to sudden priorities. It was like in the Southern when you
keyed the mike and said there was an officer down.
Down, in some cases, meaning fucked up forever, in a
cross-alley after a chase, on a warehouse floor, or reel-
ing alone around a vanished drug corner with both his
hands over his eyes. When somebody close to the mur-

der police starts crafting overtime for the murder
police, then special rules apply. This is racial. This is
an attack on every last one of us.

I badged my way through the tunnel of uniforms
around the front door, making the landlady as my best
witness or last-to-see. There was a fat full moon
reflecting the sun on to my back. Not even Italian
police are sentimental about full moons. You're looking at a workload increase of twenty-five to thirty-five
percent. A full moon on a Friday night and you're talking a two-hour backup in the emergency room and
long lines trailing in and out of Trauma.

At the door to Jennifer's apartment I was met by
Silvera. Silvera. He and myself have worked many
cases. We have stood together, like this, in many a
stricken home. But not quite like this.

"Jesus, Mike."

"Where is she?"

"Bedroom."

"You through? Wait, don't tell me. I'm going in."

The bedroom led off the living room. And I knew
where to go. Because I had been to this residence
before, maybe a dozen times in half as many years—to
drop something off for Colonel Tom, to give Jennifer a
ride to a ballgame or a beach party or a function at the
Dep Comm's. Her, and once or twice Trader, too. It was
like that, a functional kind of friendship, but with
good chats in the car. And as I crossed the living room
and leaned on the bedroom door I flashed a memory
of a couple of summers back, a party Overmars threw
after his new deck was done, when I caught Jennifer's

eye as she was smiling up from the glass of white wine she'd been nursing all night. (Everyone else apart from me, of course, was completely swacked.) I thought then that here was somebody who had a real talent for happiness. A lot of gratitude in her. I'd need a megaton of scotch to make me burn like that but she looked lovestruck on half a glass of white.

I went in and closed the door behind me.

This is how you do it. You kind of wheel around slowly into the scene. Periphery first. Body last. I mean, I knew where she was. My radar went to the bed but she had done it on a chair. In the corner, to my right. Otherwise: Curtains half-drawn against the moonlight, orderly dressing table, tousled sheets, and a faint smell of lust. At her feet, an old black-stained pillowcase and a squirt can of 303.

I have said that I am used to being around dead bodies. But I took a full hot flush when I saw Jennifer Rockwell, glazed naked on the chair, her mouth open, her eyes still moist, wearing an expression of childish surprise. The surprise light not heavy, as if she had come across something she'd lost and no longer expected to find. And not quite naked. Oh my. She'd done it with a towel turbaned around her head, like you do to dry your hair. But now of course the towel was wet through and solid red and looked as though it weighed more than any living woman could carry.

No, I didn't touch her. I just made my notes and drew my stick-figure sketch, with professional care— like I was back in the rotation. The .22 lay upside down and almost on its side, propped against the chair leg. Before I left the room I turned off the light for a second with a gloved hand and there were her eyes still moist in the moonlight. Crime scenes you look at like cartoon puzzles in the newspapers. Spot the difference. And something was wrong. Jennifer's body was beautiful—you wouldn't dare pray for a body like that—but something was wrong with it. It was dead.

Silvera went in to bag the weapon. Then the crime-lab techs would get her prints and measure distances and take many photographs. And then the ME would come and roll her. And then pronounce her.

The jury is still out on women police. On whether they can take it. Or for how long. On the other hand, maybe it's me: Maybe I'm just another fuckoff. New York PD, for instance, is now fifteen percent female. And all over the country women detectives continue to do outstanding work, celebrated work. But I'm thinking that these must be some very, very exceptional ladies. Many times, when I was in Homicide, I said to myself, *Walk away, girl. Ain't nobody stopping you. Just walk away.* Murders are men's work. Men commit them, men clean up after them, men solve them, men try them. Because men like violence. Women really don't figure that much, except as victims, and among the bereaved, of course, and as witnesses. Ten or twelve years back, during the arms buildup toward the end of Reagan's first term, when the nuclear thing was on everyone's mind, it seemed to me that the ultimate homicide was coming and one day I'd get the dispatcher's call alerting me to five billion dead: "All of them, except you and me." In full consciousness and broad daylight men sat at desks drawing up contingency plans to murder *everybody*. I kept saying out loud: "Where are the women?" Where *were* the women? I'll tell you: They were witnesses. Those straggly chicks in their tents on Greenham Common, England, making the military crazy with their presence and their stares—they were witnesses. Naturally, the nuclear arrangement, the nuclear machine, was strictly men only. Murder is a man thing.

But if there's one aspect of homicide work that women do about a thousand times better than men it's riding a note. Women are good at that—at breaking the news. Men fuck it up because of the way they always handle emotion. They always have to *act* the n.o.d., so they come on like a preacher or a town crier, or all numb and hypnotized like someone reading off a list of commodity futures or bowling scores. Then halfway through it hits them what they're doing and you can tell they're close to losing it. I've seen beat cops burst out laughing in the face of some poor little schnook whose wife just walked under a Mack truck. At such moments, men realize that they're impostors, and then anything can happen. Whereas I would say that women feel the true weight of the thing immediately and after that it's a difficult event but not an unnatural one. Sometimes, of course, *they* crack up laughing—I mean the supposedly bereaved. You're just getting into your my-sad-duty routine and they're waking up the neighbors at three in the morning to pop a party.

Well, that wasn't going to happen tonight.

The Rockwells' residence is in the northwestern suburbs, out to Blackthorn: Twenty minutes. I had Johnny Macatitch stay in the car while I went around the back way like I normally would when paying a call. I was coming by the side of the house and I paused. To step on my cigarette. To breathe. And I could see them, in through the leaded windows and past the potted plants of the kitchen, Miriam and Colonel Tom, dancing. Dancing the twist, slow, and without a whole lot of bend in the knees, to the lecherous saxophone frying like the dinner in the pan. They clinked glasses. Red wine. Up above the moon throbbed full, and the clouds it raced through seemed to be the moon's clouds rather than our clouds. Yes, an unforgettably beautiful night. And that beauty was part of this story. As if staged for my benefit, like the picture framed by the kitchen window: A forty-year marriage that still had fucking in it. Under a night so sweet it looked like day.

When you're bringing news of the kind I was bringing there are physical ramifications. The body feels concentrated. The body feels important. It has power, because it brings powerful truth. Say what you like about this news, but it's the truth. It's the truth. It is *the case*.

I rapped on the half-glass back door.

Colonel Tom turned: Pleased to see me. Not even a little frown of inconvenience, like maybe I was going to take the shine off his evening. But the instant he opened the door I could feel my face collapsing. And I knew what he thought. He thought I was back on it. I mean the booze and all.

"Mike. Jesus, Mike, are you okay?"

I said, "Colonel Tom? Miriam?" But Miriam was already falling away and fading from my sight. Falling away at thirty-two feet per second squared. "You lost your daughter on this day. You lost your Jennifer."

He looked like he was still trying to smile his way past it. The smile now starting to plead. They had David one year, Yehoshua the next. And then, a decade and a half later: Jennifer.

"Yes she's gone," I said. "By her own hand."

"This is nuts."

"Colonel Tom, you know I love you and I'd never lie to you. But it seems your baby girl took her own life, sir. Yes she did. Yes she did."

They fetched their coats and we drove downtown. Miriam stayed in the car with Johnny Mac. Colonel Tom made the ID leaning on a freezer door in the ME's office on Battery and Jeff.

Oltan O'Boye would be riding east, to campus. Taking the news to Trader Faulkner.

March 5

I woke up this morning and Jennifer was standing at the end of my bed. She was waiting for my eyes to open. I looked, and she was gone.

The ghost of a dead person must divide into many ghosts—to begin with. It is labor-intensive—to begin with. Because there are many bedrooms to visit, many sleepers to stand over.

Some sleepers—maybe just two or three—the dead will never leave.

March 6

Tuesdays I'm working the midnights. So Tuesdays I generally put in an afternoon at the Leadbetter. Attired in a taupe pants suit, I sit in my own office eighteen floors above where Wilmot deadends into Grainge. I am part-time security consultant here and I will go half-time or better when my EoD finally gets to be the mandatory twenty-five behind me. That date—my Entrance on Duty—is September 7, 1974. Retirement is already sniffing me up to see if I'm ripe.

The front desk called to say I had a visitor: Colonel Rockwell. Frankly, I was surprised that he was up and around. My understanding was that the boys were down from Chicago and the phone was off the hook. The Rockwells were digging in.

I put aside the CSSS layout I'd been staring at and I did my face. Too, I buzzed Linda, asking her to greet the elevator and bring the Colonel right on in.

He entered.

"Hey, Colonel Tom."

I stepped forward but he seemed to take a pass on the hug I was offering him and he kept his chin down as we slid off his coat. The head staying low when he sat in the leather chair. I went back of my desk and said,

"How goes it with you, Colonel Tom? My dear."

He shrugged. He exhaled slowly. He looked up.

And I saw what you seldom see in the grief-struck.
Panic. A primitive panic, a low-IQ panic, in the eyes—
it makes you consider the meaning of the word *hare-
brained*. And it made *me* panic. I thought: He's in a
nightmare and now I am too. What do I do if he starts
screaming? Start screaming? Should everybody start
screaming?

"How is Miriam?"

"Very quiet," he said, after a while.

I waited. "Take your time, Colonel," I said. I
thought it might be a good idea to do something null
and soothing, like maybe get to some bills. "Say as
much as you want or as little as you want."

Tom Rockwell was Squad Supervisor during
much of my time in Homicide. That was before he
climbed into his personal express elevator and pushed
the button marked Penthouse. In the space of ten
years he made lieutenant as Shift Commander, then
captain in charge of Crimes Against Persons, then full
colonel as head of CID. He's brass now: He isn't a
police, he's a politician, juggling stats and budgets and
PR. He could make Dep Comm for Operations. Christ,
he could make Mayor. "It's all head-doctoring and kiss-
ing ass," he once said to me. "You know what I am?
I'm not a cop. I'm a communicator." But now Colonel
Tom, the communicator, just sat there, very quietly.

"Mike. There's something went on here."

Again I waited.

"Something's wrong."

"I feel that too," I said.

The diplomatic response—but his eyes leveled in.

"What's your read on it, Mike? Not as a friend. As a police."

"As a police? As a police I have to say that it looks like a suicide, Colonel Tom. But it could have been an accident. There was the rag there, and the 303. You think maybe she was cleaning it and..."

He flinched. And of course I understood. Yeah. What was she doing with the .22 in her mouth? Maybe tasting it. Tasting death. And then she—

"It's Trader," he said. "It has to be Trader."

Well, this demanded some time to settle. Okay. Now: It is sometimes true that an apparent suicide will, on inspection, come back a homicide. But that inspection takes about two seconds. It is ten o'clock on a Saturday night, in Destry or Oxville. Some jig has just blown his chick to bits with a shotgun. But a couple of spikes later he hatches a brilliant scheme: He'll make it look like *she* did it. So he gives the weapon a wipe and props her up on the bed or wherever. He might even muster the initiative to scrawl out a note, in his own fair hand. We used to have one of these notes tacked to the squadroom noticeboard. It read: "Good By Crule Whirld." *Well this is some sad shit, Marvis,* you say when you get there, responding to Marvis's call. *What happened?* And Marvis says, *She was depress.* Discreetly, Marvis leaves the room. He's done his bit. What more can a man do? Now it's our turn. You glance at the corpse: There's no burn or shell wadding in the wound and the blood spatter is on the wrong pillow. And the wrong wall. You follow Marvis into the kitchen and he's standing there with a glassine bag in one hand and a hot spoon in the other. *Homicide. Heroin. Nice, Marvis. Come on. Downtown. Because you're a murdering piece of shit. And a degenerate motherfucker. That's why.* A homicide come dressed to the ball as a suicide: This you expect from a braindead jackboy in the Seventy-Seven. But from Trader Faulkner, Associate Professor of Philosophy of Science at CSU? *Please.* The smart murder just never happens. That's all bullshit. That's all so...pathetic. The Professor did it. Oh, sure. Murder is dumb and then even dumber. Only two things will make you any good at it: Luck and practice. If you're dealing with the reasonably young and healthy, and if the means is violent, then the homicide/suicide gray area is TV, is bullshit, is ketchup. Make no mistake, we would see it if it was there—because we *want* suicides to be homicides. We would infinitely *prefer* it. A made homicide means overtime, a clearance stat, and high fives in the squadroom. And a suicide is no damn use to anyone.

This isn't me, I thought. This isn't me, sitting here. I'm not around.

"Trader?"

"Trader. He was there, Mike. He was the last to see. I'm not saying he...But it's Trader. Trader owns her. It's Trader."

"Why?"

"Who else?"

I sat back, away from this. But then he went on, saying in his tethered voice,

"Correct me if I'm wrong. Did you ever meet anybody happier than Jennifer? Did you ever hear about anybody happier than Jennifer? More stable? She was, she was *sunny*."

"No you're not wrong, Colonel Tom. But the minute you really go into someone. You and I both know that there's always enough pain."

"There wasn't any—"

Here his voice gave a kind of hiccup of fright. And I thought he must be imagining her last moments. It took him a few swallows, and then he continued:

"Pain. Why was she naked, Mike? Jennifer. Miss Modest. Who never even owned a bikini. With *her* figure."

"Excuse me, sir, is the case being worked? Is Silvera on it? What?"

"I stetted it, Mike. It's pending. Because I'm going to ask you to do something for me."

TV, etcetera, has had a terrible effect on perpetrators. It has given them *style*. And TV has ruined American juries for ever. And American lawyers. But TV has also fucked up us police. No profession has been so massively fictionalized. I had a bunch of great lines ready. Like: *I was quit when you came in here. I'm twice as quit now*. But this was Colonel Tom I was talking to. So I spoke the plain truth.

"You saved my life. I'd do anything for you. You know that."

He reached down for his briefcase. From it he removed a folder. Jennifer Rockwell. H97143. He held it out toward me, saying,

"Bring me something I can live with. Because I can't live with this."

Now he let me look at him. The panic had left his eyes. As for what remained, well, I've seen it a thousand times. The skin is matte, containing not a watt of light. The stare goes nowhere into the world. It cannot penetrate. Seated on the other side of the desk, I was already way out of range.

"It's a little fucked up, ain't it, Colonel Tom?"

"Yeah, it's a little fucked up. But it's the way we're going to do this."

I leaned back and said experimentally, "I keep trying to think it through. You're sitting there kind of idling around with it—with the weapon. Cleaning it. Toying with it. Then a perverse thought. An infantile thought." I mean, that's how an intelligent infant finds out about something: It puts it in its mouth. "You put it in your mouth. You—"

"It wasn't an accident, Mike," he said, standing. "That's precluded by the evidence. Expect a package this time tomorrow."

He nodded at me. This package, his nod seemed to say, was going to straighten me out.

"What is it, Colonel Tom?"

"Something for your VCR."

And I thought, Oh, Jesus. Don't tell me. The young lovers in their designer dungeon. I could just see it. The young lovers, in their customized correctional facility—Trader in his Batman suit, and Jennifer shackled to her rack, wearing nothing but feathers and tar.

But Colonel Tom soon put my mind at rest.

"It's the autopsy," he said.

March 7

What with AA, golf, the Discuss Group on Mondays, and the night class on Thursdays at Pete (together with countless and endless correspondence courses), plus the Tuesday nightshift, and Saturdays, when I tend to hang with my bunkies in the Forty-Four—what with all this, my boyfriend says I don't have time for a boyfriend and maybe my boyfriend is right. But I do have a boyfriend: Tobe. He's a dear guy and I value him and I need him. One thing about Tobe—he sure knows how to make a woman feel slim. Tobe's totally enormous. He fills the room. When he comes in late, he's worse than the night train: Every beam in the building wakes up and moans. I find love difficult. Love finds me difficult. I learned that with Deniss, the hard way. And Deniss learned it too. It's this simple: Love destabilizes me, and I can't afford to be destabilized. So Tobe here suits me right down to the ground. His strategy, I suspect, is to stick around and grow on me. And it's working. But so slowly that I don't think I'll live long enough to see if it all panned out.

Tobe is no choirboy, obviously: He rooms with Detective Mike Hoolihan. But when I told him what was going to be on TV that night he took himself off to Fretnick's for a couple of cold ones. We keep booze in the apartment and somehow I like to know it's there even though it will kill me if I touch it. I cooked him an early dinner. And around seven he finished mopping up his pork chop and sloped out the door.

Right now I want to say something about myself and Colonel Tom. One morning toward the very end of my career in Homicide I came in for the eight to four—late, drunk, with a face made of orange sand, and carrying my liver on my hip like a flight bag. Colonel Tom got me into his office and said, *Mike, you can kill yourself if that's what you want. But don't expect me to watch you doing it.* He took me by the arm and led me to the second tier of the headquarters garage. He drove me straight to Lex General. The admissions doc looked me over and the first thing he said was, *You live alone, right?* And I said, *No. No, I don't live alone.* I live with Deniss...After they dried me out I convalesced at the Rockwells' residence—this was when they lived way out in Whitefield. For a week I lay in a little bedroom at the back of the ground floor. The distant traffic was music and people who weren't people—as well as people who were—came and stood at the foot of my bed. Uncle Tom, Miriam, the family physician. And then the others. And Jennifer Rockwell, who was nineteen years old, would come and read to me in the evenings. I lay there trying to listen to her clear young voice, wondering if Jennifer was real or just another of the ghosts who occasionally stopped by, cool, self-sufficient, unreproachful figures, their faces carved and blue.

I never felt judged by her. She had her troubles too, back then. And she was the daughter of a police. She didn't judge.

•   •   •

First I recheck the case folder, where you're going to find every last bit of boring shit, like the odometer reading on the unmarked that Johnny Mac and myself drove that night—the night of March fourth. But I want all the chapter and verse. I want to shore up a sequence in my mind.

19:30. Trader Faulkner is the last to see. Trader has stated that he took his leave of her at that time, as he always did on a Sunday night. Jennifer's apparent mood is described here as "cheerful" and "normal."

19:40. The old lady in the attic apartment, dozing in front of her TV, is woken by a shot. She calls 911.

19:55. Beat cop shows. The old lady, Mrs. Rolfe, keeps a set of spare keys to Jennifer's apartment. Beat cop gains access and finds body.

20:05. Tony Silvera takes the call in the squad-room. The dispatcher gives the name of the victim.

20:15. I am summoned by Detective Sergeant John Macatitch.

20.55. Jennifer Rockwell is pronounced.

And twelve hours later she is cut.

TACEANT COLLOQUIA, it says on the wall. EFFUGIAT RISUS. HIC LOCUS EST UBI MORS GAUDET SUCCURRERE VITAE.

Let talking cease. Let laughter flee. This is the place where death delights to help the living.

Die suspiciously, die violently, die unusually—in fact, die pretty much anywhere outside an intensive-care unit or a hospice—and you will be cut. Die unattended, and you will be cut. If you die in *this* American city, the paramedics will bring you down to the ME's office on Battery and Jefferson. When it's time to get around to you there, you will be trolleyed out of the walk-in freezer, weighed, and rolled onto a zinc gurney under an overhead camera. It used to be a microphone, and you'd take Polaroids. Now it's a camera. Now it's TV. At this stage your clothes will be examined, removed, bagged, and sent to Evidence Control. But Jennifer is wearing nothing but a toe-tag.

And it begins.

Maybe I'd better point out that the process itself, for me, means close to nothing. When I worked homicides, the autopsy room was part of my daily routine. And I still get down there on business at least once a week. Asset Forfeiture, which is a subdivision of Organized Crime, is a lot more hands-on than it sounds. Basically what we do is: We rip off the Mob. One whisper of conspiracy, out there by the pool, and we confiscate the entire marina. So we deal with bodies. Bodies found, almost always, in the trunks of airport rental cars. Impeccably executed and full of bullets. You're down in the ME's office half the morning sometimes, on account of all the bullets they have to track...The process itself doesn't mean much to me. But Jennifer does. I am confidently assuming that Colonel Tom didn't watch this, and would have relied on Silvera's summary. Why am I watching it? Take away the bodies, and the autopsy room is like the kitchen of a restaurant that has yet to open. I am watching. I am sitting on the couch, smoking, taking notes, and using the Pause. I am bearing witness.

Silvera is there: I can hear him briefing the pathologist. Jennifer is there, wearing her toe-tag. That body. The scene photographs in the case folder, with the moist eyes and mouth, could almost be considered pornographic (arty and "tasteful"—kind of *ecce femina*), but there's nothing erotic about her now, stiff like out of the deepfreeze, and flat on a slab between striplights and tiles. And all the wrong colors. The chemistry of death is busy with her, changing her from alkaline to acid. *This is the body...* Wait. That sounds like Paul No. Yes, the cutter is Paulie No. I guess you can't blame a guy for loving his job, or for being Indonesian, but I have to say that that little slope gives me the creeps. This is the body, he is saying, echoing the sacrament: *Hoc es corpus*.

"This is the body of a well-developed, well-nourished white female, measuring five feet ten inches in height and weighing approximately one hundred and forty pounds. She is wearing nothing."

First the external examination. Directed by Silvera, No takes a preliminary look at the wound. He shines a light into the mouth, which is rigored half open, and rolls her on to her side to see the exit. Then he scans the entire epidermis for abnormalities, marks, signs of struggle. Particularly the hands, the fingertips. No takes nail clippings, and performs the chemical tests for barium, antimony and lead deposits—to establish that she fired the .22. I recall that it was Colonel Tom who bought her that gun, years back, and taught her how to use it.

Brisk as ever, Paulie No takes oral, vaginal and anal swabs. Too, he inspects the perineal area for tearing or trauma. And again I'm thinking of Colonel Tom. Because this is the only way that his read works. I mean, for Trader to be involved, it has to be a sex deal, right? Has to be. And it feels all wrong. Some funny things can happen on the cutter's table. A double suicide can come back a homicide-suicide. A rape-murder can come back a suicide. But can a suicide come back a rape-murder?

Autopsy is rape too, and here it comes. In the moment that the first incision is made, Jennifer becomes all body, or body only. Paul No is going in now. Goodbye. The elevation makes him look like a school child, glossy head dipped, and the scalpel poised like a pen as he makes the three cuts in the shape of a Y, one from each shoulder to the pit of the stomach, and then on down through the pelvis. Up come the flaps—it makes me think of a carpet being lifted after damage by flood or fire—and No goes through the ribs with the electric saw. The breastplate comes out like a manhole lid and then the organ tree is removed entire (the organ tree, with its strange fruit) and placed in the steel sink to the side. No vivisects heart, lungs, kidneys, liver, and takes tissue samples for analysis. Now he's shaving the head, working in toward the exit wound.

But here's the worst. The electric saw is circumnavigating Jennifer's cranium. A lever is being wedged

under the roof of the skull, and now you wait for the
pop. And now I find that *my* body, so ordinary and
asymmetrical, the source of so little pleasure or pride,
so neglected, so parched, is suddenly starting up, acting up: It wants attention. It wants out of all this. The
cranial pop is as loud as a gunshot. Or a terrible
cough. No is pointing to something, and Silvera leans
forward, and then the two men are backing away, in
surprise.

I watch on, thinking: Colonel Tom, I hear you.
But I'm not sure how much this means.

It appears that Jennifer Rockwell shot herself in
the head three times.

No. No, I don't live alone, I said. I live with Deniss. And
just that once I shed tears. I don't live alone. I live with
Deniss.

As I was speaking those words, Deniss, in actual
fact, was scowling through the windscreen of a U-
Haul, taking himself and all his belongings at high
speed toward the state line.

So I did live alone. I didn't live with Deniss.

Is that Tobe now, starting up the stairs? Or is it
the first rumor of the night train? The building always
seems to hear it coming, the night train, and braces
itself as soon as it hears in the distance that desperate
cry.

I don't live alone. I don't live alone. I live with
Tobe.

March 9

Just come back from my meet with Silvera.

The first thing he said to me was: "I hate this."

I said you hate what?

He said the whole damn thing.

I said Colonel Tom thinks it plays to homicide.

He said what does?

I said the three shots.

He said Rockwell never was any good. On the streets.

I said he got shot in the line for Christ's sake. He got shot in the fucking line.

Silvera paused.

"When was the last time *you* took one for the state?" I asked him.

Silvera went on pausing. But that wasn't it. He wasn't thinking of the time, way back in company lore, that Tom Rockwell stopped one in the Southern, as a beat cop, while flushing hoodies from a drug corner. No, Silvera was just contemplating his own career curve.

I lit a cigarette and said, "Colonel Tom has it playing to homicide."

He lit a cigarette and said, "Because that's all he's got. You shoot yourself once in the mouth. That's life. You shoot yourself twice. Hey. Accidents happen. You shoot yourself three times. You got to really want to go."

We were in Hosni's, the little gyro joint on Grainge. Popular among police for its excellent smoking section. Hosni himself isn't a smoker. He's a libertarian. He threw out half his tables just to skirt city law. I'm not proud of my habit, and I know that Hosni's crusade is one we're eventually going to lose. But all cops smoke their asses off and I figure it's part of what we give to the state—our lungs, our hearts.

Silvera said, "And this was a .22. A revolver."

"Yeah. Not a zip. Or a faggot gun. You know like a derringer or something. The old lady upstairs. She said she heard one shot?"

"Or she's woken by one shot and then hears the second or the third. She's blacked out on sherry in front of the TV. What does *she* know."

"I'll go talk to her."

"This case is so fucking cute," said Silvera. "When Paulie No fluoroscoped her, suddenly we're looking at three bullets. One's still in her head, right? One's in Evidence Control: The one we dug out of the wall at the scene. After the autopsy we go back. There's only one hole in the wall. We dig out *another* round. Two bullets. One hole."

In itself this was no big deal. Police are pretty blasé about ballistics. Remember the Kennedy assassination and "the magic bullet"? We know that every bullet is a magic bullet. Particularly the .22 roundnose. When a bullet enters a human being, it has hysterics. As if it knows it shouldn't be there.

I said, "I've seen twice. In suicides. I can imagine three."

"Listen, I've *chased* guys who've taken three in the head."

The truth was we were waiting on a call. Silvera

had asked Colonel Tom to let Overmars in on this. Seemed like the obvious guy, with his Quantico connections. And right now Overmars was stirring up the federal computers, looking for documented three-in-the-head suicides. I was finding it kind of a weird calculation. Five in the head? Ten? When were you *sure*?

"What you get this morning?"

"Nothing but schmaltz. What you get?"

"Yeah, right."

Silvera and myself had also been working the phones that morning. We'd called everybody who was likely to have an opinion about Jennifer and Trader, as a couple, and we'd both compiled the same dimestore copy about how they seemed to have been made for each other—in heaven. There was, to put it mildly, no evidence of previous gunplay. So far as anyone knew, Trader had never raised his voice, let alone his fist, to Jennifer Rockwell. It was embarrassing: Sweet nothings all the way.

"Why was she nude, Tony? Colonel Tom said Miss Modest never even owned a bikini. Why would she want to be found that way?"

"Nude is the least of it. She's dead, Mike. Hell with nude."

We had our notebooks open on the table. There were our sketches of the scene. And Jennifer drawn as a stick figure: One line for the torso, four lines for the limbs, and a little circle for the head, at which an arrow points. A stick figure. Was *that* ever inadequate.

"It says something."

Silvera asked me what.

"Come on. It says I'm vulnerable. It says I'm a woman."

"It says get a load of this."

"Playmate of the Month."

"Playmate of the Year. But it's not that kind of body. More of a sports body with tits."

"Maybe we're coming in at the end of a sex thing here. Don't tell me that didn't occur to *you*."

Be a police long enough, and see everything often enough, and you will eventually be attracted to one or another human vice. Gambling or drugs or drink or sex. If you're married, all these things point in the same direction: Divorce. Silvera's thing is sex. Or maybe his thing is divorce. My thing, plainly, was drink. One night, near the end, a big case went down and the whole shift rolled out to dinner at Yeats's. During the last course I noticed everybody was staring my way. Why? Because I was blowing on my dessert. To cool it. And my dessert was ice cream. I was a bad drunk, too, the worst, like seven terrible dwarves rolled into one and wedged into a leather jacket and tight black jeans: Shouty, rowdy, sloppy, sleazy, nasty, weepy, and horny. I'd enter a dive and walk up the bar staring at each face in turn. No man there knew whether I was going to grab him by the throat or by the hog. And I didn't know either. It wasn't much different at CID. By the time I was done, there wasn't a cop in the entire building who, for one reason or the other, I hadn't slammed against a toilet wall.

Silvera is younger than me and the wheels are coming off his fourth marriage. Until he was thirty-five, he claims, he balled the wife, girlfriend, sister and mother of every last one of his arrests. And he certainly has the look of the permanent hardon. If Silvera was in Narcotics, you'd right away make him for dirty: The fashionably floppy suits, the touched-up look around the eyes, the Italian hair trained back with no part. But Silvera's clean. There's no money in murder. And a hell of a detective. Fuck yes. He's just seen too many movies, like the rest of us.

"She's naked," I said, "on the chair in her bedroom. In the dark. There are times when a woman will willingly open her mouth to a man."

"Don't tell Colonel Tom. He couldn't handle it."

"Or play this. Trader leaves at 19:30. As usual. And then her *other* boyfriend shows."

"Yeah, in a jealous rage. Listen, you know what Colonel Tom is trying to do."

"He wants a who. I tell you this. If it's a suicide, I'm going to feel an awful big why."

Silvera looked at me. Police really are like footsoldiers in this respect at least. Ours not to reason why. Give us the how, then give us the who, we say. But fuck the why. I remembered something—something I'd been meaning to ask.

I said you make a pass at anything that stirs, right?

He said oh yeah?

I said yeah. If your rash isn't acting up. You ever try Jennifer?

He said yeah, sure. With someone like that you

got to at least *try*. You'd never forgive yourself if you didn't at least *try*.

I said and?

He said she brushed me off. But nicely.

I said so you didn't get to call her an icebox or a dyke. Or religious. Was she religious?

He said she was a scientist. An astronomer. Astronomers aren't religious. Are they?

I said how the hell would I know?

"Would you put that cigarette out, please, sir?"

I turned.

Guy says, "Excuse me. Ma'am. Would you put that cigarette out, please, ma'am?"

This is happening to me more and more often: The sir thing. If I introduce myself over the phone it never occurs to anybody that I'm not a man. I'm going to have to carry around a little pack of nitrogen or whatever—the stuff that makes you sound like Tweetie Bird.

Silvera lit a cigarette and said, "Why would she want to put her cigarette out?"

Guy's standing there, looking around for a sign. Big guy, fat, puzzled.

"See that booth behind the glass door," said Silvera, "with all those old files heaped up in it?"

Guy turns and peers.

"That's the no-smoking section. If what you're interested in is having people put their cigarettes out, you might find more play in there."

Guy slopes off. We're sitting around, smoking,

and drinking the cowboy coffee, and I said hey. In the old days. Did *I* ever throw a pass at *you*? Silvera thought about it. He said as far as he remembered, I just slapped him around a few times.

"March fourth," I said. "It was O'Boye notified Trader, right?"

On the night of the death, Detective Oltan O'Boye drives out to CSU to inform Professor Trader Faulkner. The deal is, Trader and Jennifer cohabit, but every Sunday night he takes to his cot in his office on campus. O'Boye is banging on his door around 23:15. Trader is already in pajamas, robe, slippers. Notified of his loss, he expresses hostile disbelief. There's O'Boye, six feet two and three hundred pounds of raw meat and station-house dough fat in a polyester sport coat, with an alligator complexion and a Magnum on his hip. And there's the Associate Professor, in his slippers, calling him a fucking liar and getting ready to swing his fists.

"O'Boye brought him downtown," said Silvera. "Mike, I've seen some bad guys in my time, but this one's a fucking beauty. His eyeglasses are as thick as the telescope at Mount Lee. And get this. He had *leather patches* on the elbows of his tweed jacket. And there he sits on a bench in the corridor, bold as day, crying into his hands. Son of a bitch."

I said he see the body?

He said yeah. They let him see her.

I said and?

He said he kind of leaned over it. Thought he was going to hold her but he didn't.

I said he say anything?

He said he said Jennifer...Oh, Jennifer, what have you done?

"Detective Silvera?"

Hosni. And Overmars's call. Silvera rose, and I started gathering our stuff. Then I gave him a minute before joining him by the phone.

"Okay," I said. "How many three-in-the-heads we got?"

"It's great. Seven in the last twenty years. No problem. We got a four-shot too."

On our way to the door we took a glance at the no-smoking section. The guy was in there, alone, unattended, unserved, looking vigilant and strained.

"He's like Colonel Tom," said Silvera. "He's in the wrong section. Oh and guess what. Five of them were women. It's like we say. Men kill other people. It's a guy thing. Women kill themselves. Suicide's a babe thing, Mike."

March 10

Saturday. In the morning, just for the hell of it, really, I do a half-block canvass on Whitman Avenue. It's a nice neighborhood now. A middle-class enclave on the frontier of the Twenty-Seven: You got the old University Library over on Volstead, and the Business School on York. American cities like to fix it so that their seats of learning are surrounded by war zones (this is reality, pal), and it used to be that way around here. Ten years ago, Volstead Street was like the Battle of Stalin-

grad. Now it's all nailed up and scorched-looking—
vacated or plain abandoned, with hardly a hoody in
sight. It's tough to say who made this happen. The
economy did it.

So as I move from door to door, under the elms,
the residents are very, very cooperative. It wasn't like
doing a rowhouse block in Oxville or a project in
Destry. Nobody told me to go suck cocks in hell. But
nobody saw anything either. Or heard anything, on
March fourth.

Until my last call. Yeah. Wouldn't you know. A little girl, too, in pink ribbons and bobby socks. Silvera's
right: This case is so fucking cute. But it's not pure
ketchup, because kids do notice things, with their new
eyes. The rest of us just looking out there and seeing
the same old shit.

I'm winding it up with the mom, who suddenly
says, "Ask Sophie. Sophie! Sophie was out riding her
new bike up and down the street. I don't let her leave
the street on it." Sophie comes into the kitchen and I
hunker down on her.

Now, honey, this could be important.

"Number 43. Yeah. The one with the cherry tree."

Think carefully, sweetheart.

"My chain came loose? I was trying to fix the
chain?"

Go on, honey.

"And a man came out?"

What did he look like, sweetheart?

"Poor."

Poor? Honey, what do you mean? Like shabby?

"He had patches on his clothes."

It took me a second. He had patches on his *elbows*. Poor. That's right: Don't they say the darnedest things?

Sweetheart. How'd he seem?

"He looked mad. I wanted to ask him to help me but I didn't."

And soon I'm saying, "Thanks, honey. Thanks, ma'am."

When I badge my way from door to door like this, and the women see me coming up the path—I don't know what they think. There I am in my parka, my black jeans. They think I'm a diesel. Or a truck driver from the Soviet Union. But the men know at once what I am. Because I give them the eyeball— absolutely direct. As a patrol cop, on the street, that's the first thing you have to train yourself to do: Stare at men. In the eyes. And then when I was plainclothes, and undercover, I had to train myself out of it, all over again. Because no other kind of woman on earth, not a movie star, not a brain surgeon, not a head of state, will stare at a man the way a police stares.

Back home I field the usual ten messages from Colonel Tom. He veers around, racking his brains for shit on Trader. A prior record of instability and temper-loss that amounts to a few family disagreements and a scuffle in a bar five years ago. Examples of impatience, of less than perfect gallantry, around Jennifer. Times he let her walk by a puddle without dunking his coat in it.

Colonel Tom is losing the story line. I wish he could hear how he sounds. Some of his beefs are so smallprint, they make me think of diss murders. Diss murders: When someone gets blown in half for a breach of form that would have slipped by Emily Post.

"What's the game plan, Mike?"

I told him. Jesus...Anyway, he seemed broadly satisfied.

If the jury is still out on women police, then the jury is still out on Tobe. Still out, after all these months, and still hollering for transcripts of the judge's opening address.

Right now the guy is next door watching a *taped* quiz show where the contestants have been instructed beforehand to jump up and down and scream and whoop and french each other every time they get an answer right. The multiple-choice questions do not deal in matters of fact. They deal in hearsay. The contestants respond, not with what they think, but with what they think everybody else thinks.

I just went through and sat on the great couch of Tobe's lap for five minutes and watched them doing it. Grown adults acting like five-year-olds at a birthday party, with this routine:

What do Americans think is America's favorite breakfast? Cereal. *Boing.* Only 23 percent. Coffee and toast? Whee! All *right.*

What do Americans think is America's choice suicide method. Sleeping pills. Yeah! Ow!

Where do Americans think France is? In Canada. *Get* down!

March 11

There's an obit in this morning's Sunday *Times*. In its blandness and brevity you can feel the exertion of all Tom Rockwell's heft.

Just a resumé, plus manner of death ("as yet undetermined"). And a photograph. This must have been taken, what, about five years ago? She is smiling with childish lack of restraint. Like you'd just told her something wonderful. If you skimmed over this photograph—the smile, the delighted eyes, the short hair emphasizing the long neck, the clean jaw—you'd think that here was someone who was about to get married kind of early. Not someone who had suddenly died.

Dr. Jennifer Rockwell. And her dates.

The little girl on Whitman, with her pink ribbons and bobby socks? She didn't *hear* anything, on March fourth. Today, however, I went to see someone who did.

Mrs. Rolfe, the old dame on the top floor. It's half after five and she's half in the bag. So I don't expect much. And I don't get much. It's sweet sherry she's drinking: The biggest bang for the buck. Mr. Rolfe died many years ago and she's quietly splashing her way through a widowhood that's lasting longer than her marriage.

I ask about the shots. She says she was dozing (yeah, right), and the TV was on, and there were shots on the TV also. Some cop thing, naturally. She describes the report she heard for definite as unmistakably a gunshot, but no louder than a door being slammed two or three rooms away. You can feel the weight of the building: Constructed in an age of cheap materials. Mrs. Rolfe dialed 911 at 19:40. First officer showed at 19:55. Plenty of time, theoretically, for Trader to pack up and split. The little girl wheeled her bike in "around a quarter of eight," according to her mother. Which puts Trader on the street—when? 19:30? 19:41?

"They fight ever?"

"Not to my knowledge, no," says Mrs. Rolfe.

"How'd they seem to you?"

"Like the dream couple."

But what kind of dream?

"It's just so awful," she says, making a move for the sauce. "It's shaken me up, I admit."

I used to be like that. Any bad news would do. Like your friend's friend's dog died.

"Mrs. Rolfe, did Jennifer seem depressed ever?"

"Jennifer? She was always cheerful. Always cheerful."

Trader, Jennifer, Mrs. Rolfe: They were neighborly. Jennifer ran errands for her. If she needed something heavy shifted, Trader would shift it. They kept a spare key for her. She kept a spare key for them. She still had that spare key, used to gain access on the night of March fourth. I say I'll take that key, thank you, ma'am, and log it with Evidence Control. Left her my card, in case she needed anything. I could see myself looking in on her here, as I still do for several elderly parties in the Southern. I could see myself developing an obligation.

On the floor below: The door to Jennifer's apartment is sashed with orange crime-scene tape. I slipped inside for a second. My first reaction, in the bedroom, was strictly police. I thought: What a beautiful crime scene. Totally undeteriorated. Not only the blood spatter on the wall but the sheets on the bed have the exact same pattern that I remember.

I sat on the chair with my .38 on my lap, trying to imagine. But I kept thinking about Jennifer the way she used to be. As gifted as she was, in body and mind, she never glassed herself off from you. If you ran into her, at a party, say, or downtown, she wouldn't say hi and move on. She'd always be particular with you. She'd always leave you with something.

Jennifer would always leave you with something.

March 12

Today my shift was noon to eight. Sitting there smoking cigarettes and changing tapes, changing tapes— audio, visual, audiovisual. We're casing the new hotel in Quantro, because we know the Outfit has money in it. I finally got the visual fix I was looking for: Two guys in the atrium, standing in the shadows back of the fountain. When we say the Outfit or the Mob, in this city, we don't mean the Colombians or the Cubans, the Yakuza, the Jake posses, the El Ruks, the Crips and the Bloods. We mean Italians. So I watched these two beaners in blue suits that cost five grand, gesturing at each other, very formal. Men of honor, worthy of respect. Wise guys had long before stopped behaving that way, but then some movies came along that reminded them that their grandparents used to do that shit, with the honor, and so they started doing it, all over again.

Incidentally: We want that hotel.

I feel grateful for quiet workloads on days such as this, days of lethargy and faint but persistent nausea which have to do with my time of life, and my liver. More my liver than my unused womb. My only way around this is a transplant, a full organ transplant, which is possible, and expensive. But the precariousness—the risk of hepatic collapse—keeps me honest. If I bought a new liver, I'd just trash that one too.

Early afternoon Colonel Tom buzzed me and asked if I'd come up to his office on the twenty-third.

He is shrinking. His desk is big anyway but now it looks like an aircraft carrier. And his face like a little gun turret, with its two red panic buttons. He isn't getting better.

I told him the move I planned for Trader.

You'll go in hard, he said. Like I know you can.

Like you know I can, Colonel Tom.

Freestyle, Mike, he said. Flake him. I don't care if he spills and walks. I just want to hear him say it.

To hear him say it, Colonel Tom?

I just want to hear him say it.

With Silvera or Overmars, you could always tell when a case was beating them down: They started shaving every other day. That, plus the usual symptoms of being wide awake for a month. Pretty soon they're like the guys gathered around the braziers in the stockyards sidings—ghosts of a Depression section gang, lit by the flares...Colonel Tom's cheeks were smooth. His cheeks were smooth. But he couldn't take a razor to the brown smears of pain beneath his eyes which were deepening and hardening like scabs.

"Don't buy all that Ivy League, Skull and Bones bullshit. The soft voice. The logic. Like even *he* thinks he's too good to be true. There's evil in him, Mike. He..."

Falling silent. His head vibrated, his head actually trembled to terrible imaginings. Imaginings he wanted and needed to be true. Because any outcome, yes, any at all, rape, mutilation, dismemberment, cannibalism, marathon tortures of Chinese ingenuity, of Afghan lavishness, any outcome was better than the other thing. Which was his daughter putting the .22 in her mouth and pulling the trigger three times.

Colonel Tom was now going to lay something on me. I could feel it coming. He roused himself. Briskly but also ditheringly, he leafed through a binder: Looked like a lab report out of the ME's office. I wondered how Colonel Tom was monitoring and controlling the post-mortem findings as they came in piece by piece.

"Jennifer tested positive for ejaculate, vaginal and oral," he said—and it was costing him to go on looking my way. "Oral, Mike. You see what I'm saying?"

I nodded. And of course I was thinking, Jesus, this really *is* fucked up.

Eight days on and Jennifer Rockwell is still laid out like a banquet dish in the walk-in freezer on Battery and Jeff.

March 13

Time for Trader.

My first thought was this: I'd send Oltan O'Boye and maybe Keith Booker up to Trader's department at CSU, in a black-and-white, and have them jerk him out of a seminar. Yeah, with lights but no sirens. Have them yank him out of the lecture hall or wherever, and bring him downtown. The hitch was we'd be up against probable cause way too early. And whatever Colonel Tom thought we had, we didn't have probable cause.

So I just called his room on campus. At six A.M.

"Professor Faulkner? Detective Hoolihan. Homicide. I want you downtown today at Criminal Investigations. As soon as you humanly can."

He said what for?

"I'll send the wagon. You like me to send the wagon?"

He said what for?

And I just said I wanted to straighten some things out.

In truth it's perfect for me.

Around eight in the morning, and we're three hours into a blizzard that has upped and hurled itself down from Alaska. You got hail, sleet, snow, and spume skimmed off from the ocean, plus face-slapping gouts of iced rain. Trader will be trudging along from the subway stop or clambering out of a cab down there on Whitney. He'll look up, for shelter, at the Lubianka of CID. Where he will find a succession of drenched and dirty linoleum corridors, a slow-climbing, heavy-breathing elevator, and, in Homicide, a forty-four-year-old police with coarse blonde hair, bruiser's tits and broad shoulders, and pale blue eyes in her head that have seen everything.

And Trader will find hardly anybody else. It's Tuesday. In Homicide the zoo contains only a smattering of witnesses, suspects, malefactors and perpetrators. The *weekend*, which for us is just a code word meaning a regular bender of citywide crime, has come and gone. And there is also the bad weather: Bad weather is the big police. For company, while he waits in the zoo, Trader will have only the husband, the father and the pimp of a bludgeoned prostitute, and a Machine executioner (presently top of the money list) called Jackie Zee who has been asked downtown to elaborate on an alibi.

The phones are silent. The midnight shift is

falling apart and the eight-to-four is limping in. Johnny Mac is reading an editorial in *Penthouse*. Keith Booker, big black motherfucker with scars and whole gold ingots on most of his teeth, is trying to watch a college ballgame from Florida on the faulty TV. O'Boye is painfully bent over his typewriter. These guys are kind of in on it. Only Silvera has the full picture, but these guys are kind of in on it. Trader Faulkner will be receiving no words of condolence from anybody here.

At 08:20 the Associate Professor checks in downstairs and is shunted up to the fourteenth. I watch him step out. In his right hand he is holding his briefcase, in his left the pink card issued him by building security at the front desk. The rim of his fedora, which has lost its definition in the rain, is starting to droop over his darkened face, and his overcoat gives off a faint vapor under the tube lighting. His gait is deliberate and kind of wide at the knees. His inturned shoes are squelching toward me.

He says, "It's Mike, isn't it. Good to see you again."

And I say, "You're late."

Johnny Mac gives him a leer, and Detective Booker does a good job of chewing gum in his direction, as Trader is led into the zoo. I point to a chair. And walk away. If he likes, Trader can talk philosophy with Jackie Zee. A half-hour later I return. In response to a wag of my head Trader gets to his feet and I reescort him back past the elevators.

At this point, as arranged, Silvera strolls out of the door marked Sex Crimes and says hey Mike, what we got?

And I say something like: We got the dead hooker that was turning ten-dollar dates in AllRight Parking. We got that murdering asshole Jackie Zee. And we got *this*.

Silvera looks Trader up and down and says need any input?

And I say nah. And I mean it. This will be the sum total of Silvera's participation. None of that good cop–bad cop bullshit, which doesn't work anyway. It's not just that Joe Perp is on to it, having seen good cop–bad cop a million times on reruns of *Hawaii Five-O*. The fact is that since the Escobedo ruling, which was thirty years ago, bad cop has lost all his moves. The only time bad cop was any good was in the old days, when he used to come into the interrogation room every ten minutes and smash your suspect over the head with the Yellow Pages. And besides: I had to do this alone and in my own way. It's how I've always worked.

I turned, and preceded Trader Faulkner to the small interrogation room, pausing only to slide the key off its nail.

Overdoing it slightly, maybe, I locked him up alone in there for two and a half hours. I did say he could bang on the door if he wanted anything. But he never stirred.

Every twenty minutes I go and take a look at him through the mesh window, which of course is a one-way. All he sees is a scratched and filmy mirror. What

I see is a guy of around thirty-five in a tweed jacket with leather patches sewn on to his elbows.

Axiom:

Left alone in an interrogation room, some men will look as though they're well into their last ten seconds before throwing up. And they'll look that way for hours. They sweat like they just climbed out of the swimming pool. They eat and swallow air. I mean these guys are really going through it. You come in and tip a light in their face. And they're bug-eyed—the orbs both big and red, and faceted also. Little raised soft-cornered squares, wired with rust.

These are the innocent.

The guilty go to sleep. Especially the veteran guilty. They know that this is just the dead time that's part of the deal. They pull the chair up against the wall and settle themselves in the corner there, with many a grunt and self-satisfied cluck. They crash out.

Trader wasn't sleeping. And he wasn't twitching and gulping and scratching his hair. Trader was *working*. He had a thick typescript out on the table beside the tin ashtray and he was writing in corrections with a ballpoint, his head bent, his eyeglasses milky under the bare forty-watt. An hour of this, then two hours, then more.

I go in and lock the door behind me. This trips the tape recorder housed beneath the table where Trader sits. I feel a third party in the room: It's like Colonel Tom is already listening in. Trader's looking up at me with patient neutrality. From under my arm I take the

case folder and toss it down in front of him. Clipped to
its cover is a five-by-eight of Jennifer dead. Beside it I
place a sheet headed Explanation of Rights. I begin.

> Okay. Trader. I want you to answer some
> background questions. That's fine by you,
> right?
> I guess so.
> You and Jennifer were together for how
> long?

Now he keeps *me* waiting. He takes off his glasses and
measures up his gaze to mine. Then he turns away. His
upper teeth are slowly bared. When he answers my
question he seems to have to move past an impediment. But not an impediment of speech.

> Almost ten years.
> You two met how?
> At CSU.
> She's what? Seven years younger?
> She was a sophomore. I was a postdoc.
> You were teaching her? She was your stu-
> dent?
> No. She was math and physics, I was phi-
> losophy.
> Explain it to me. You do philosophy of sci-
> ence, right?
> I do now. I switched. Back then I was
> doing linguistics.

Language? Philosophy of language?

That's right. Conditionals, actually. I spent all my time thinking about the difference between "if it was" and "if it were."

And what do you spend all your time thinking about now, friend?

...Many worlds.

Excuse me? You mean other planets?

Many worlds, many minds. The interpretation of relative states. Popularly known as "parallel universes," Detective.

Sometimes I have the look of a grave child trying not to cry. I have it now, I know. As with the child, staying dry-eyed while enduring sympathy, it's more like defiance than self-pity. When I don't understand something, it makes me feel defiant. I feel: I will not be excluded from this. But of course you are excluded, all the time. You just have to let it go.

So it wasn't an academic connection. You met how?

...Socially.

And you moved in together when?

When she graduated. About eighteen months later.

How would you characterize your relationship?

Trader pauses. I light a cigarette with the butt of its predecessor. As usual, and of set purpose, I am

turning the interrogation room into a gas chamber.
For-hire executioners, bludgeoners of prostitutes—
they seldom object to this (though you'd be surprised).
A professor of philosophy, I reckoned, might have
lower tolerance. That's sometimes all you're left with
in here: The full ashtray. Buts and butts, we call it.
You're left with the full ashtray, and the rising levels in
your lungs.

Could I take one of those?

Go ahead.

Thanks. I quit. When I moved in with Jennifer, actually. We both quit. But I seem to
have started again. How would I characterize our relationship? Happy. Happy.

But it was winding down.

No.

There were problems.

No.

Okay. So everything was great. We'll leave
it like that for a minute.

Excuse me?

You guys were building for the future.

Such was my understanding.

Get married. Kids.

Such was my understanding.

You two talked about it...I asked if you
talked about it...Okay. Kids. You wanted
kids? You yourself?

...Sure. I'm thirty-five. You begin to want
to see a fresh face.

She want them?

She was a woman. Women want children.

He looks at me, my town flesh, my eyes. And he's thinking: Yeah. All women except this woman.

You're saying women want children in a different way? Jennifer wanted children in a different way?

Women want children physically. They want them with their bodies.

They do, huh? But you don't.

No, I just think that if you're going to live life...

To the full...

No, if you're going to live it at all. Then the whole deal, please. Could I...?

Go ahead.

I now had to purge myself of the last traces of affability. Not a big job, some would say. Tobe might say it, for instance. A police works a suspicion into a conviction: That's the external process. But it's the internal process also. It is for me. It's the only way I can do it. I have to work suspicion into conviction. Basically I have to get married to the idea that the guy did it. Here, I have to become Colonel Tom. I have to buy it. I have to want it. I have to *know* the guy did it. I know. I know.

Trader, I want you to take me through the events of March fourth. This is what I'm doing, Trader. I want to see if what you give me measures up to what we have.

To what you have?

Yes. Our physical evidence from the crime scene, Trader.

From the crime scene.

Trader, you and myself live in a bureaucracy. We have some bullshit to get through here.

You're going to read me my rights.

Yes, Trader. I'm going to read you your rights.

Am I under arrest?

This amuses you. No, you're not under arrest. You want to be?

Am I a suspect?

We'll see how you do. This sheet—

Wait. Detective Hoolihan, I can end this, can't I. I don't have to tell you anything. I can just call a lawyer, right?

You feel like you need a lawyer? You feel like you need a lawyer, hey, we can whistle one up. Then that's it. This case binder goes to the assistant state's attorney and I can't do a damn thing for you. You feel like you need a lawyer? Or you want to sit here with me and straighten this whole thing out.

Again Trader bares his teeth. Again the look of difficulty, of impediment. But now he gives a sudden nod and says,

Begin. Begin.

This sheet is headed Explanation of Rights. Read and sign and initial each section. There. And there. Good. Okay. Sunday. March fourth.

Trader lights another cigarette. By now the small interrogation room is split-level with smoke. He leans forward and begins to speak, not dreamily or wistfully but matter-of-fact, his arms folded, his eyes dipped.

Sunday. It was Sunday. We did what we always do on Sunday. We slept late. I got up around ten-thirty and made breakfast. Scrambled eggs. We read the *Times*. You know how it is, Detective. Bathrobes. Her with the Arts, me with the Sports. We did an hour's work. We went out just before two. We walked around. We had a beef sandwich at Maurie's. We walked around. Around Rodham Park. It was a beautiful day. Cold and bright. We played tennis, indoors, at the Brogan. Jennifer won, as always. The score was 3–6, 6–7. We got back around five-thirty. She made lasagne. I packed a bag—

You're damn right you packed a bag.

I don't understand you. We always spent Sunday nights apart. It was Sunday. I packed a bag.

You're damn right you packed a bag.

Because this was no ordinary Sunday, was it, Trader. Had you felt it coming? For how long? You were losing her, weren't you, Trader. She wanted out from under you, Trader, and you could feel it. Maybe she was already seeing somebody else. Maybe not. But it was over. Oh, come on, man. It's everyday. You know how it is, Professor. There are popular songs about it. Get on the bus, Gus. Drop off the key, Lee. But you weren't going to let that happen, were you, Trader. And I understand. I understand.

Untrue. Not the case. False.

You said her mood that day was what?

Normal. Cheerful. Typically cheerful.

Yeah, right. So after a typically cheerful day with her typically cheerful boyfriend, she waits until he leaves the house and puts two bullets in her head.

Two bullets?

That surprises you?

Yes. Doesn't it surprise you, Detective?

In the past, I have come into this interrogation room with damper ammo than I had on me now, and duly secured a confession. But not often. Men accused of wholesale slaughter, and not for the first time, proven killers with rapsheets as long as toilet rolls: Such men I have coated in sweat with nothing more than a single Caucasoid hair strand or half a Reebok footprint. It's simple. You do them with science. But science was what Trader was a philosopher of.

I am going to go in hard now. No quarter.

Trader, at what point did you and the decedent have sex?

What?

The decedent tested positive for ejaculate. Vaginal and oral. When did that happen?

None of your business.

Oh it *is* my business, Trader. It's my job. And I'm now going to tell you exactly what happened that night. Because I know, Trader. I know. It's like I was *there*. You and her have the final argument. The final fight. It's over. But you wanted to make love to her that one last time, didn't you, Trader. And a woman, at such a moment, will let that happen. It's human, to let that happen. One more time. On the bed. Then on the chair. You finished on the chair, Trader. You finished it. And fired the shot into her open mouth.

Two shots. You said two shots.

Yes I did, didn't I. And now I'm going to tell you a secret that you already know. See this? This is the finding from the autopsy. Three shots, Trader. Three shots. And let me tell you, that *wipes out* suicide. That *wipes out* suicide. So Mrs. Rolfe upstairs did it, or the little girl in the street did it. Or you did it, Trader. Or you did it.

The space around him goes gray and damp, and I feel the predator in me. He looks drunk—no, drugged. Like on speed: Not hammered but "blocked." I would understand, later, what was happening in his head: The image that was forming there. I would understand because I would see it too.

It was the look on his face made me ask him:

> How do you feel about Jennifer? Right now? Right this minute?
> Homicidal.
> Come again?
> You heard me.
> Good, Trader. I think we're getting there. And that's how you felt on the night of March fourth. Wasn't it, Trader.
> No.

All the hours I have spent in the interrogation room, over the years, are stacking up on me, I feel, all the hours, all the fluxes and recurrences of the heaviest kinds of feeling. It's the things you have to hear and keep on hearing: From your own lips, also.

> I have a witness that puts you outside the house at seven thirty-five. Looking distressed. "Mad." Riled-up. Sound familiar, Trader?
> Yes. The time. And the mood.
> Now. My witness says she heard the shots before you came out the door. Before. Sound about right, Trader?

Wait.

Okay. Sure I'll wait. Because I understand. I understand the pressure you were under. I understand what she was putting you through. And why you had to do what you did. Any man might have done the same. Sure I'll wait. Because you won't be telling me anything I don't already know.

With its tin ashtray, its curling phonebook, its bare forty-watt, the interrogation room doesn't have the feel of a confessional. In here, the guilty man is not seeking absolution or forgiveness. He is seeking approval: Grim approval. Like a child, he wants out of his isolation. He wants to be welcomed back into the mainstream—whatever he's done. I have sat on this same honky metal chair and routinely said, with a straight face—no, with indignant fellow feeling: *Well that explains it. Your mother-in-law had been sick for* how *long without dying? And you're supposed to take* that *lying down?* I have sat here and said: *Enough is enough. You're telling me the baby woke up crying* again? *So you taught it a lesson. Sure you did. Come on, man, how much shit can you take?* Give Trader Faulkner a reversed baseball cap, a stick of gum, and a bad shave, and I would be leaning forward over the table and saying, again, absolutely as a matter of rou-tine: *It was the tennis, wasn't it. It was that fucking tiebreak. The* lasagne *was as lousy as ever. And then she rounds it all off by giving you* that *kind of head?*

I cross myself inside and vow to go the extra mile for Colonel Tom—and give it a hundred percent, like I always do.

Take your time, Trader. And consider this, while you think. Like I said, we've all been there, Trader. Think it hasn't happened to me? You give them years. You give them your life. The next thing you know, you're on the street. She used to tell you she couldn't live without you. Now she's saying you ain't even shit. I can understand how it feels to lose a woman like Jennifer Rockwell. You're thinking about the men who'll be taking your place. And they won't be slow in coming. Because she was hot, wasn't she, Trader. Yeah, I know the type. She'll fuck her way through your friends. Then she'll get to your brothers. In the sack she'll soon be doing them those nice favors you know all about. And she would, Trader. She would. Now listen. Let's reach the bottom line. Dying words, Trader. The special weight, as testimony, of dying words.

What are you saying, Detective?

I'm saying the dispatcher's call came through at nineteen thirty-five. We reached the scene minutes later. And guess what. She was still there, Trader. And she named you. Anthony Silvera heard it. John Macatitch

heard it. I heard it. She gave you up. How
about that, Trader? There. The cunt even
gave you up.

We have been in here for fifty-five minutes. His
head is down. As evidence, a confession will tend to
lose its power in step with the length of the interrogation. Yes, your honor—after a couple of weeks in there,
he came clean. But I am mentally ready to go on for six
hours, for eight, for ten. For fifteen.

Say it, Trader. Just say it...Okay, I'm
going to ask you to submit to a neutron-
activation test. This will establish if you have
recently used a firearm. Will you sit the poly-
graph? The lie-detector? Because I think you
ought to know what the next stage is in all
this. Trader, you're going before a grand jury.
Know what that is? Yes, I'm going to *grand-
jury* you, Trader. Yes I am...Okay. Let's start
from the beginning. We're going to go
through all this a few more times.

He looks up slowly. And his face is clear. His
expression is clear. Complicated, but clear. And suddenly I know two things. First, that he's innocent. Second, that if he wants to, he can prove it.

As it happens, Detective Hoolihan, I do
know what a grand jury is. It's a hearing to
establish whether a case is strong enough to

go to trial. That's all. You probably think I think it's the Supreme Court. Same as all the other befuddled bastards that come through here. This is so...pathetic. Oh, Mike, you poor bitch. Listen to you. But it's not Mike Hoolihan talking. It's Tom Rockwell. And the poor sap ought to blush for what he's just put you through. It's also kind of great—I mean, this whole thing is also kind of great. Last week I sat down with maybe ten or twelve people, one after the other. My mother, my brothers. My friends. Her friends. I kept opening my mouth and nothing happened. Not a word. But I'm talking now and let's please go on talking. I don't know how much you've told me is just plain bullshit. I'm assuming the ballistics document is not a hoax or a forgery and I'll have to live with what it says. Maybe you'll be good enough to tell me now what's true and what isn't. Mike, you've tied yourself up into all kinds of knots trying to make a mystery of this thing. It's garbage, as you know. Some little mystery, all neat and cute. But there's a real mystery here. An enormous mystery. When I say I feel homicidal, I'm not lying. On the night she died my feelings were what they always were. Devoted, and secure. But now...Mike, this is what happened: A woman fell out of a clear blue sky. And you know something? I wish I *had* killed her. I want to say: Book me. Take me away. Chop my head off. I wish I had killed her. Open and shut. And no holes. Because that's better than what I'm looking at.

If you peered in now, through the meshed glass, it wouldn't seem such a strange way for things to end, in this room. Glimpsing this scene, a murder police would nod his head, and sigh, and move on.

Suspect and interrogator have joined hands on the table. Both are shedding tears.

I shed tears for him and tears for her. And also tears for myself I shed. Because of the things I've done to other people in this room. And because of the things this room has done to me. It's pulled me into every kind of funny shape and size. It has left a coating on my body, everywhere, even inside, like the coating I used to expect to see, some mornings, all over my tongue.

March 14

I slept late and was woken around noon by another delivery from Colonel Tom. A dozen red roses—"with thanks, apologies, and love." Also a sealed binder. Expedited, and very probably edited, by Colonel Tom, this was the autopsy report. I'd seen the movie. Now I had to read the review.

It took a couple of pots of coffee and half a package of cigarettes before I could swim free of the liver haze that had come down on me during the night, like gruel. I showered also. And it must have been close to two before I sat myself down on the couch in my terrycloth bathrobe. I have this tape I like that Tobe made up for me: Eight different versions of "Night Train." Oscar Peterson, Georgie Fame, Mose Allison, James Brown. We think of it as a kind of hymn to the low rent. The rent's nothing: I mean, you don't notice it. You notice the night train but you don't notice the rent. So I had that playing, softly, in the corner, as I wrenched at the red tape. Spend ten years fucked up, spend ten years blowing on your ice cream, and you're going to have a ten-year hangover (with another twenty-some waiting in line). Which is not to say that I wasn't feeling all the extra from the day before. I felt fat and butter-colored, and already sweaty or still damp from the bathroom haze.

Haec est corpus. This is the body:

Jennifer, your height was five-ten, your weight 141.

Your stomach contained a fully digested meal of scrambled eggs, lox, and bagels, and another meal, only partly digested, of lasagne.

Lividity was only where it ought to have been. No one moved your body. No one arranged you.

Blowback. On your right hand and forearm were found microscopic particles of blood and tissue. We call this *blowback*.

Too, your right hand had undergone cadaveric spasm. Or spontaneous, and temporary, rigor mortis. The curve of the trigger and the patterning of the butt were embedded in your flesh. That's how tight you gripped.

Jennifer, you killed yourself.

It's down.

March 16

At CID, people aren't talking about it. Like we took a beating on this one. But everyone now knows for sure that Jennifer Rockwell committed a crime on the night of March fourth.

If she'd slid into the car and driven a hundred miles due south to the state line, then she could have died innocent. In our city, though, what she did was a crime. It's a crime. The perfect crime, as always, in a way. She didn't escape detection. But she escaped all punishment.

And she escaped public disgrace. If disgrace is what you want to call it. Ask the coroner, who absolved her.

Go far enough back, and a coroner was just a tax collector. To stay with the Latin of death: *Coronae custodium regis.* Keeper of the king's pleas. He taxed the dead. And suicides lost all they had. Like other felons.

These days, in this city, the coroner works out of the Chief Medical Examiner's office. His name is Jeff Bright and he's a pal of Tom Rockwell's.

Bright returned a finding of Undetermined. Colonel Tom, I know, pushed for Accidental. But he settled for Undetermined, as we all did.

I said I never felt judged by her, even when I was defenseless against all censure. And, as of this writing, I feel no need to judge Jennifer Rockwell. With suicide, as with all the great collapses, exits, desertions, surrenders, it gets so there isn't any choice.

And there's always enough pain. I keep thinking back to that time when I was holed up at the Rockwells' house, sweating out my soul into the bedding. She too had her troubles. At nineteen—slimmer, gawkier, wider-eyed—she too was under siege. I remember now. One of those late-adolescent convulsions, with the parents pacing. There was a spurned boyfriend who wouldn't or couldn't let go. Yes, and a girlfriend too (what was it—drugs?), a housemate of hers, who'd also flipped out. Jennifer would give a jolt every time the phone or the doorbell rang. But yet, as sad and scared as she was, she would come and read to me and tend to me.

She didn't judge me. And I don't judge her.

Here's what happened. A woman fell out of a clear blue sky.

Yes. Well. I know all about these clear blue skies.

March 18

At the funeral, then, no color guard, no twenty-one-gun salute, no bagpipes. A couple of white hats, some gold braid and chest candy, and the full church service, with the little gray guy in his vestments whose language was saying: *We* take over now. Commit her to us, to this—the green fields and the church in the middle distance, its spire pointing heavenward. No, this wasn't a police occasion. We were outnumbered. There we all stood, with our dropped eyes and our shared defeat, surrounded by an army of civilians: It seemed like the whole campus was in attendance. And I had never seen so many youthful and well-proportioned faces made hideous by grief. Trader was there, close to the family group. His brothers stood beside Jennifer's brothers. Tom and Miriam faced the grave, motionless, like painted wood.

Earth, receive the strangest guest.

In the Dispersal Area I slipped away toward the yews for a dab of makeup and a cigarette. Grief brings out the taste of cigarettes, better than coffee, better than booze, better than sex. When I turned again I saw that Miriam Rockwell was approaching me. Under her black headscarf she looked like a beautiful beggar from the alleys of Casablanca or Jerusalem. Beautiful, but definitely asking, not giving. And I knew then that her daughter wasn't done with me yet. Not by a damn sight.

We held each other—partly for the warmth,

because the sun itself felt cold that day, like a ball of yellow ice, chilling the sky. With Miriam, physically, there seemed to be a little less of her to heft in your arms, but she wasn't obviously reduced, scaled down, like Colonel Tom (standing some distance off, waiting), who looked about five feet three. Less crazy, though. Sadder, more sunken, but less crazy.

She said, "Mike, I think this is the first time I've seen your legs."

I said, "Well enjoy." We looked down at them, my legs, in their black hose. And it felt okay to say, "Where did Jennifer get her legs from? Not from you, girl. You're like me." Jennifer's legs belonged to some kind of racehorse. Mine are like road drills on castors. And Miriam's aren't a whole lot better.

"I used to say, let her for the rest of her life wonder where she got her figure from. Let her try to piece it together. Her figure and her face. The legs? From Rhiannon. From Tom's mother."

There was a silence. Which I lived intensely, with my cigarette. This was my moment of rest.

"Mike. Mike, there's something we now know about Jennifer that we want you to know about too. You ready for this?"

"I'm ready."

"You didn't see the toxicology report. Tom made it disappear. Mike, Jennifer was on *lithium*."

Lithium...I absorbed it—this lithium. In our city, in Drugburg here, a police quickly gets to know her pharmaceuticals. Lithium is a light metal, with commercial applications in lubricants, alloys, chemical reagents. But lithium carbonate (I think it's a kind of salt) is a mood stabilizer. There goes our clear blue sky. Because lithium is used in the treatment of what I have heard described (with accuracy and justice) as the Mike Tyson of mental disorders: Manic depression.

I said, "You never knew she had any kind of problem like that?"

"No."

"You talk to Trader?"

"I didn't tell Trader. With Trader I kind of talked around it. But no. No! Jennifer? Who do you know as steady as her?"

Yeah, but people do things without people knowing. People kill, bury, divorce, marry, change sex, go nuts, give birth, without people knowing. People have triplets in the bathroom without people knowing.

"Mike, it's funny, you know? I'm not saying it's any better. But with this we turned some kind of corner."

"Colonel Tom?"

"He's back. I thought we'd lost him there. But he's back."

Miriam swiveled. There he stood, her husband: The heavy underlip, the scored orbits. Like *he* was on lithium now. His mood was stabilized. He was gazing, steadily, through the universal fog.

"See, Mike, we were looking for a why. And I guess we found one. But suddenly we don't have a who. Who was she, Mike?"

I waited.

"Answer that, Mike. Do it. If not you, who? Henrik Overmars? Tony Silvera? Take the time. Tom'll push you some compassionate. Do it. It has to be you, Mike."

"Why?"

"You're a woman."

And I said yes. I said yes. Knowing that what I'd find wouldn't be any kind of Hollywood ketchup or bullshit but something absolutely somber. Knowing that it would take me through my personal end-zone and all the way to the other side. Knowing too—because I think I did know, even then—that the death of Jennifer Rockwell was offering the planet a piece of new news: Something never seen before.

I said, "You're sure you want an answer?"

"Tom wants an answer. He's a police. And I'm his wife. It's okay, Mike. You're a woman. But I think you're tough enough."

"Yeah," I said, and my head dropped. I'm tough enough. And getting less proud of it every hour.

She turned again toward the waiting figure of her husband, and slowly nodded. Before she moved to join him, and before I followed with my head still down, Miriam said,

"Who the hell was she, Mike?"

I think we all have this image in our heads now, and the sounds. We have these frames of film. Tom and

Miriam have them. I have them. In the small interrogation room I watched them form on the other side of Trader's eyes—these frames of film that show the death of Jennifer Rockwell.

You wouldn't see her. You'd see the wall behind her head. Then the first detonation, and its awful flower. Then a beat, then a moan and a shudder. Then the second shot. Then a beat, a gulp, a sigh. Then the third.

You wouldn't see her.

PART TWO

FELO DE SE

THE PSYCHOLOGICAL AUTOPSY

Suicide is the night train, speeding your way to darkness. You won't get there so quick, not by natural
means. You buy your ticket and you climb on board.
That ticket costs everything you have. But it's just a
one-way. This train takes you into the night, and leaves
you there. It's the night train.

Now I feel that someone is inside of me, like an
intruder, her flashlight playing. Jennifer Rockwell is
inside of me, trying to reveal what I don't want to see.

Suicide is a mind-body problem that ends violently and without any winner.

I've got to slow this shit down. I've got to slow it
all down.

What I'm doing here, with my ballpoint, my tape
recorder, and my PC—it's the same as what Paulie No
was doing in the ME's office, with his clamp, his electric saw, his trayfull of knives. Only we call it the psychological autopsy.

I can do this. I am trained to do this.

Recall:

For a time, though only a short time, and only once to my face, they used to call me "Suicide Mike." This was thought to be too offensive, even for downtown, and they soon abandoned it. Offensive not to the poor bastards found slumped in carseats in sealed garages, or half submerged in crimson bathtubs. Offensive to me: It meant I was fool enough to take any bum call. Because a suicide didn't do a damn thing for your solve rate or your overtime. On the midnights the phone would ring and Mac or O'Boye would be pouting over the cupped receiver and saying, *How about you handle this one, Mike? It's an s.d. and I need dough for my mother's operation.* A suspicious death— not the murder he craves. For little-boy-lost here also believes that suicides are an insult to his forensic gifts. He wants a regular *perpetrator.* Not some schmuck who, a century ago, would have been buried at the four-corners, under a heap of rocks, with a stake through his heart. Then for a time—a short time, as I say—they'd hold out the phone and deadpan, *It's for you, Mike. It's a suicide.* And then I'd yell at them. But they weren't wrong, maybe. Maybe it moved and compelled me more than it did them, to crouch under the bridge on the riverbank, to stand in a rowhouse stairwell while a shadow rotated slowly on the wall, and think about those who hate their own lives and choose to defy the terrible providence of God.

As part of my job I completed, as many others did, the course called "Suicide: Harsh Conclusions," at Pete, and followed that up, again on city time, with the refresher lecture series on "Patterns of Suicide," at CC.

I came to know the graphs and diagrams of suicide, their pie segments, their concentric circles, their color codes, their arrows, their snakes and ladders. With my Suicide Prevention tours, back in the Forty-Four, plus the hundred-some suicides I worked in the Show, I came to know not just the physical aftermaths but the basic suicide picture, ante mortem.

And Jennifer doesn't belong here. She doesn't belong.

I have my folders out on the couch, this Sunday morning. Going through my notes to see what I got:

- In all cultures, risk of suicide increases with age. But not steadily. The diagonal graph-line seems to have a flattish middle section, like a flight of stairs with a landing. Statistically (for what stats are worth around here), if you make it into your twenties, you're on level ground until the risk bump of the midlife.
  Jennifer was twenty-eight.

- About 50 percent of suicides have tried before. They are parasuicides or pseudosuicides. About 75 percent give warning. About 90 percent have histories of egression—histories of escape. Jennifer hadn't tried before. So far as I know, she did not give warning. All her life she saw things through.

- Suicide is very, very means-dependent. Take the means away (toxic domestic gas, for instance) and the rate plummets.

Jennifer didn't need gas. Like many another
American, she owned a gun.

- These are my notes. What about *their* notes, and
  what percentage leave them? Some studies say
  70 percent, others say 30. Suicide notes, it is
  assumed, are often spirited away by the
  decedent's loved ones. Suicides, as we have seen,
  are often camouflaged—smudged, snowed.
  Axiom: Suicides generate false data.
  Jennifer, apparently, did not leave a suicide note.
  But I know she wrote one. I just feel
  this.

It may run in families but it's not inherited. It is a
pattern, or a configuration. It's not a predisposition. If
your mother kills herself, it won't help, and it opens a
door...

Here are some other do's and don'ts. Or don'ts,
anyway:

Don't work around death. Don't work around
pharmaceuticals.

Don't be an immigrant. Don't be a German, just
off the boat.

Don't be Romanian. Don't be Japanese.

Don't live where the sun doesn't shine.

Don't be an adolescent homosexual: One in three
will attempt.

Don't be a nonagenarian Los Angelean.

Don't be an alcoholic. It's suicide on the install-
ment plan, anyway.

Don't be a schizophrenic. Disobey those voices in your head.

Don't be depressed. Lighten up.

Don't be Jennifer Rockwell.

And don't be a man. Don't be a man, whatever you do. Tony Silvera was, of course, talking through his ass when he said that suicide was "a babe thing." To the contrary, suicide is a dude thing. *Attempting* is a woman thing: They're more than twice as likely to do that. *Completing* is a man thing: They're more than twice as likely to do that. There's only one day in the year when it's safer to be male. Mother's Day.

Mother's Day is the day for *felo de se*. How come? I wonder. Is it the all-you-can-eat brunch at the Quality Inn? No. The suicides are the women who skipped the lunch. They're the women who skipped the kids.

Don't be Jennifer Rockwell.

The question is: But why not?

STRESSORS AND PRECIPITANTS

The first person I'm going to be wanting to talk to is Hi Tulkinghorn—Jennifer's physician. Over the years I've come across this old party a bunch of times at the Rockwells' (barbecues, cocktails on Christmas Eve). And, recall, Colonel Tom had him in to look me over, when I was drying out there: DT-ing for a week in one of the children's bedrooms on the first floor. Which I don't remember a whole lot about. Small, bald, clean-eyed, Tulkinghorn's the kind of elderly medic who, over time, seems to direct more and more of his doctoring know-how inward—to keep his own little show on the road. The *other* kind of elderly medic is a drunk. Or *he's* drying out. When I was drying out, Jennifer used to come into the room in the evenings. She'd sit in the corner and read to me. She'd feel my brow and fetch me water.

Now. I had called Tulkinghorn's office on March eighth, almost two weeks ago. And how about this. The old prick was on a *poker cruise* in the Caribbean. So I had his secretary page him and he came squawking in from *The Straight Flush*. Told him the news and said I was following up on it. He said to make an appointment. I called his office again, and got talking. It turned out that it isn't Tulkinghorn who plays poker. It's his wife. He gets nice and tan on a lounger—while she's crouching at a table in the saloon, blowing the second home on her two pair.

Hi Tulkinghorn works out of a gothic apartment block near Alton Park, over in the Thirty-Seven. I sat there in the narrow corridor, like a patient, with an ear-sufferer on one side of me and a throat-sufferer on the other. The parched secretary sat in her cubbyhole pushing paper around and answering the phone: "Doctor's office?" Younger guys in smocks, like interns, sloped in and out with clipboards and vials. Walls of folders and binders, floor to ceiling: What? Fading biopsy reports. Dust-coated urinalyses. Mr. Ear and Mr. Throat both groaned raggedly when the woman nodded me through. I passed from the corridor shadows into the Germanic tang of Tulkinghorn's surgery and the usual smell of mouthwash.

I'd like to be able to say that Hi's tan made him look like death warmed up. But he just twinkled away, self-sufficiently enough, there behind his desk. Now, this I do remember. When I was hallucinating, in the little room at Colonel Tom's, visited by visitors, some of them real, some of them not, and wondering how the hell I was going to get through the next half hour, I'd sometimes think: I know. I'll fuck one of these ghosts. That'll kill some time. But I didn't want to fuck Hi Tulkinghorn. He has too much death knowledge, soberly absorbed, in his pale blue eyes. Careful here. Don't say Hi.

"Doctor."

"Detective. Take a seat."

"How was the cruise? Your wife make money?"

"She broke about even. I'm sorry I missed the funeral. I tried to get a flight from Port of Spain. I've talked with Colonel and Mrs. Rockwell. I'll be doing what I can there."

"Then you know why I'm here."

We paused. I opened my notebook and looked down at the page. I was suddenly very impressed by my jottings of the night before. Which said: *Nature of the disorder: Reactive/non-reactive? Affective/ideational? Psychological/organic? From within or without?* I began:

Dr. Tulkinghorn, what kind of patient was Jennifer Rockwell?

...She—she wasn't.

Excuse me? What was her medical history?

She didn't have one.

I don't follow.

As far as I'm aware she never had a day's illness in her life. Except of course in infancy. Her checkups were a joke.

When was the last time you saw her?

Saw her here? About a year ago.

Was she under the care of anybody else?

I'm not sure I understand. She had a dentist, and a gynecologist, a Dr. Arlington. She's a friend of mine. Same story there. As a specimen Jennifer was close to phenomenal.

Then why was she on lithium, Doctor?

Lithium? She was not on lithium, Detective.

See this? This is Toxicology. She have a psychiatrist?

Certainly not. I'd have been notified—you know that.

He took the Xeroxed sheet from my hand and surveyed it with indignation. With quiet indignation. I knew what he was thinking. Already, he was thinking: If she didn't get it from a professional, then where did she get it? The next thought being: You can get anything in this city—easy. Yeah, tell me about it. And not from a hoody on a corner but from a smiling piece of shit in a labcoat. The names of the drugs out there can run on for twenty-five syllables...A silence followed. A silence of the kind that must be pretty frequent, in his line of work. In delivery rooms, over test results, in the

reflected light of X-ray screens. And then Dr. Tulkinghorn gave up on Jennifer. With the slightest flex of his
shoulders, he let Jennifer Rockwell go.

Yes, well. At least you're getting a pattern here. She
was medicating her own head. That's always delusional.

How so?

It's like mental hypochondria. Psychotropic drugs
would tend to intensify that. You'd get a spiral effect.

Tell me, Doc: How surprised were you when you
heard?

Surprised. Surprised. Oh, sure. And I was sick for
Tom and Miriam. But at my age. In this profession. I'm
not sure I'm capable...of astonishment.

And I wanted to say: *You* guys kill yourself a lot,
don't you. You do: Your rate is three times higher than
Joe Shmoe's. Shrinks top the list at six times higher.
Then, in descending order, you got vets, pharmacists,
dentists, farmers, and doctors. What's the connection
here, I wonder. Exposure to the natural processes of
death, disease, and decay, maybe. Or just exposure to
suffering—often dumb suffering. And availability of
means. The studies talk about "role strain." But police
have role strain too. And although we're prone to suicide, we're nothing like these fucking kamikazes in their
sky-blue smocks. Retirement time sees all of us most at
risk. I think it's to do with power. With the daily exercise
of power and what happens to you when it's taken away.

I looked up from my notes. Something shifted in
Tulkinghorn's focus. He contemplated me. I was no
longer his interrogator. I was Detective Mike Hooli-

han, whom he knew: A police and an alcoholic. And a patient. His washed eyes now regarded me with approval, but a cold approval, one that gave no lift to the spirit. To his or to mine.

"You've kept yourself in shape, Detective."

"Yes, sir."

"No recurrences of that nonsense."

"None."

"Good. You've seen just about everything too, haven't you?"

"Just about. Yes, sir, I believe I have."

When I got back home I dug out the list I'd compiled on my return from the funeral. Briskly, boldly, this list is headed, Stressors and Precipitants. But what follows now seems vague as rain:

1. Significant Other? Trader. Things he didn't see?

2. Money?

3. Job?

4. Physical Health?

5. Mental Health? Nature of disorder:

   a. psychological?

   b. ideational/organic?

   c. metaphysical?

6. *Deep* Secret? Trauma? Childhood?

7. *Other* Significant Other?

Now I cross out 4. Which leaves me wondering what I mean by 5 c). And thinking about 7. Is Mr. Seven her lithium connect?

A SENSE OF AN ENDING

Death scenes are as delicate as orchids. Like death chemistry itself, they seem committed to the business of deterioration and decay. But my death scene has eternal youth. It still has the sash on the door. Do Not Cross. I cross.

The blood on the bedroom wall looks black now, with just the faintest undercoat of rust. At the top of the splatter, near the ceiling, the smallest drops gather like tadpoles, their tails pointing away from the site of the wound. A rectangular section of the wall has been removed by the science team, right in the middle of the base smear, where the bullet hole was. Then the downward swipe from the wedged towel.

I think of Trader, and find that I am contemplating the scene as largely an interior-decoration problem. I want to get out the mop and make a start on it myself. When he returns, will he be able to sleep in this room? How many licks of paint will he want? Surprisingly, I think I am finding a friend in Trader Faulkner. Barely a week after I tried my level best to flake him into the lethal injection, I am finding a friend in Trader Faulkner. I talked with him at the wake at the Rockwells'. It is his key I hold in my hand. He has told me where to look for everything.

Jennifer kept all her personal papers in a locked

blue trunk in the living area, and I have a key for that too. But first I quickly cover the apartment from room to room, just to get a feel: Post-its on the mirror above the telephone, magnetic Scrabble pieces on the fridge door (saying MILK and FILTERS), a bathroom cabinet containing cosmetics and shampoos and a few patented medicines. In the bedroom closet her sweaters are stacked in plastic covers. Her underwear drawer is a galaxy—star-bright…

It used to be said, not so long ago, that every suicide gave Satan special pleasure. I don't think that's true—unless it isn't true either that the Devil is a gentleman. If the Devil has no class at all, then okay, I agree: He gets a bang out of suicide. Because suicide is a mess. As a subject for study, suicide is perhaps uniquely incoherent. And the act itself is without shape and without form. The human project implodes, contorts inward—shameful, infantile, writhing, gesturing. It's a mess in there.

But I look around now and what I'm seeing is settled order. Tobe and myself are both slobs, and when a pair of slobs shack up together you don't get slob times two—you get slob squared. You get slob cubed. And this place, to me, feels like a masterpiece of system: Grooved, yet unemphatic, with nothing rigid in it. Homes of the self-slaughtered have a sullen and defeated aspect. The abandoned belongings seem to say: Weren't we good enough for you? Weren't we any good? But Jennifer's apartment looks as though it is expecting its mistress to return—to fly in through the door. And against all expectation I start to be happy.

After weeks with a sour twist in my gut. The building is freestanding and even after a half hour you can feel the sun moving around it and changing the angles of all the shadows.

Trader and Jennifer, they had two bureaus, two work stations, in the living room, not ten feet apart. On his desk there is a sheet of typing paper with stuff like this written on it:

$$p(x) = a_0 + a_1 x + a_2 x^2 + a_3 x^3 + \ldots$$

On her desk there is a sheet of typing paper with stuff like this written on it:

$$x = \tfrac{30}{10^{-2}T} m = 3 \times 10^{22} m.$$

And you think, Hey. He heard her. She heard him. They talked the same language. Isn't that what we're all supposed to want? The peer lover, ten feet away: Silence, endeavor, common cause. Isn't that what we're all supposed to want? For him a woman in the room. For her a man in the room, ten feet away.

I popped the blue trunk.

It contained nine photo albums and nine rib-boned bundles of letters—all of them from Trader. This is their history, illustrated and annotated. And of course ordered. Ordered especially or ordered anyway? With a premeditated suicide there is generally some kind of half-assed attempt "to put things in order": To attempt completion. To try for completion. But I didn't get that vibe here, and figured that the

Trader "shrine" had been up and running since year one. I hauled it all out and got myself down there on the rug. Starting at the beginning: His first letter, or note, is dated June 1988:

> *Dear Ms. Rockwell: Forgive me, but I couldn't*
> *help noticing you on Court Two this afternoon.*
> *What a beautiful all-court game you have—*
> *and what a toreador backhand! I wonder if*
> *sometime I could prevail upon you to give me*
> *a game, or a lesson. I was the dark-haired,*
> *bow-legged hacker on Court One.*

And so it proceeds ("That was quite a set of tennis!"), with little memos about lectures and lunches. Soon the album is taking up the story: There they are on the court, individually and then together. Then complication. Then complication falling away. Then sex. Then love. Then vacations: Jennifer in a ski suit, Jennifer on the beach. Man, what a bod: At twenty, she looked like a model in an ad for those cereals that taste great but also make you shit right. Bronzed Trader at her side. Then graduation. Then cohabitation. And still the handwritten letters keep coming, the words keep coming, the words a woman wants to hear. No dashed-off faxes from Trader. Faxes, which fade in six months, like contemporary love. No scrawled reminders propped against the toaster, such as I get from Tobe. And used to get from Deniss, from Jon, from Shawn, from Duwain. GET SOME TOILET

PAPER FOR CHRIST SAKE. That wouldn't do for Jennifer. She got a fucking poem every other day.

Complication? Complication fell away, and did not recur. But complication there certainly was. Its theme: Mental instability. Not hers. Not his. Other people's. And I have to say that I was very, very surprised to see my own name featuring here...

I prepared myself for what they're now calling a "segue." But a lot of this stuff I already knew. The dumped boyfriend. The freaked-out flatmate. The trouble begins at the outset, when Trader starts getting serious. There's this jock, name of Hume, who has to be eased out of the picture. Big Man on Campus can't take the strain. So what he does is present Jennifer with the spectacle of his collapse. Et cetera. Then the other problem, unconnected to this or to anything else in the outside world: A roommate of Jennifer's, a girl called Phyllida, wakes up one morning with black smoke coming out of her ears. Suddenly this nerdy little chick is either gaping at the bathroom wall or out there howling at the moon. Jennifer can't cope with being around her, and bolts, back to the Rockwell home. And who does she find there, stinking up her brother's bedroom and babbling at the pillows, but Detective Mike Hoolihan. "Jesus Christ," Trader quotes her as saying, "I'm surrounded."

Here's a frustration with a one-way correspondence. The narrative doesn't "unfold": What you get is just a jumping status quo. Astonishing developments simply and smugly become How Things Are. Still,

Trader spends a lot of ink on Jennifer around now, coaxing her out of the notion that nobody and nothing can be trusted. Sanity, or at least logic, returns. You can finish the stories:

The boyfriend, Hume, drops out for a time, and does some drugs. But he's readmitted, and comes through civilized. He and Jennifer even manage an okay lunch.

Thickly sedated, Phyllida gets to graduate. Some collateral family member takes her in. References to her are frequent for a while. Then trail away.

And Mike Hoolihan recovers. It is approvingly noted that even someone with a background such as hers can eventually patch things together, with the right kind of understanding and support.

While Trader and Jennifer, of course, watch these heavy clouds pass over and cruise on up into their clear blue sky.

Now the bureaus and the filing cabinets and the endless, endless shite of citizenship, of existence. Bills and wills, deeds, leases, taxes—oh, man, the water torture of staying alive. *That's* a good reason to end it. Confronted with all this, who wouldn't want to rest and sleep?

Two hours on my knees brings me only two mild surprises. First: Trader, on top of everything else, is a man of independent means. I seem to remember that his daddy was big in the construction business during the Alaska boom. Here, anyway, is Trader's modest portfolio—his bonds and shelters, his regular and generous donations to charity. Second: Jennifer never opened her bank statements. The fiercest-looking wallets of crap from the IRS lie wrenched open on her desk—but she never opened her bank statements. Here they all are, backed up from last November, and still sealed. Well, I soon rectify that. And find prudent outgoings plus a nice little sum on deposit. So why not read this good news? Then I get it. She never opened her statements because she never had to do anything about them. These were letters that needed no answer. That's what you call a sufficiency. That's putting dough in its proper place.

What to me feels the most intimate thing I have saved till last. Her worn leather handbag, left slung over the shoulder of a kitchen chair. This shoulder is like her shoulder, erect, wide-spanned, with the gentlest inward curve…Jesus, *my* bag, which I seem to spend half my life scrabbling around in, is like a town dump that's gone through a car compactor. I've no idea what's going on in there. Mice and mushrooms flourish among the fenders and spare tires. But Jennifer, naturally, traveled light, and fragrant. Boar's bristle hairbrush, moisturizer, lip gloss, eyedrops, blush. Pen, purse, keys. Also, her datebook. And if what I'm looking for is a sense of an ending, then here I get it big-time.

I flick the pages. Jennifer wasn't the kind of busybody who faced a thicket of commitments every waking hour. But for the first two months of the year there's plenty happening—appointments, schedules, deadlines, reminders. And then on March second, the Friday, it all stops dead. There is nothing else for the whole year, except this, under March 23: "AD?" Which is tomorrow. Who or what is AD? Advertisement? Anno Domini? I don't know—Alan Dershowitz?

Before I left, as I was closing the blue trunk, I took another look at Trader's last letter. It was among the loose papers and photos yet to be gathered and organized, and it was dated February 17, this year. The postmark says Philadelphia, where Trader was attending a two-day conference on "The Mind and Physical Laws." It's almost embarrassing: I can hardly bring myself to quote from it. "Already the eastern side of every moment of mine is lit by you and the thought of tomorrow..."

I love you. I miss you. I love you. No. Jennifer Rockwell didn't have a problem with this boyfriend. He's perfect. He's everything we all want. So what I'm thinking now is she must have had a problem with the *other* boyfriend.

Photograph on a bookcase. It's graduation: Jennifer and three friends in gowns, all tall but bent with laughter. Laughing so hard they look fucked up on something. And the little crazy one, Phyllida, trapped in the frame, cowering in the corner of it.

Funny thing about the apartment. It took me a while to realize what.

No TV.

And a funny thought, on the way out. Suddenly I'm thinking: But she's a cop's daughter. This means something. This has to matter.

• • •

Like all police I guess I'm state-of-the-art cynical, on the one hand. And, on the other, I don't judge. We never judge. We may make the roust and make the collar. We may bust you. But we won't judge you.

Fresh from the latest slaughterhouse, that kraut brute Henrik Overmars will listen to a drunk's hard-luck story with tears in his eyes. I've seen Oltan O'Boye give his last fin to some self-pitying asshole at Paddy's—some guy whose entire acquaintance has drawn down the shade on him, years ago. Keith Booker can't pass a bum on the street—no, every time he'll slip him a buck and squeeze his hand. I'm the same way. We're the softest touch.

Is it because we're plain brutal/sentimental? I don't think so. We don't judge you, we can't judge you because whatever you've done it isn't even close to the worst. You're great. You didn't fuck a baby and throw it over the wall. You don't chop up eighty-year-olds for laughs. You're great. Whatever you've done, we know all the things you *might* have done, and *haven't* done.

In other words, our standards, for human behavior, are desperately low.

Having said all that, I was due for a shock tonight. I felt what I so seldom feel: Scandalized. I felt *shock* all over my body. Forget about a hot flush. I practically had the menopause in one fell swoop.

I'm back at the apartment, cooking dinner for

Tobe and myself. The phone goes and a male voice says,

"Yeah, can I speak with Jennifer Rockwell please?"

I said, in receptionist singsong, "Who's calling?"

"Arnold. It's Arn."

"One moment!"

I'm standing there tensed in the kitchen heat. Tell myself to work on what I was doing already: Keep your voice pitched up. Sound like a woman.

"Actually—hello again—actually Jennifer's out of town tonight and I'm handling her messages here. I have her datebook here. Hey, were you guys meant to get together tomorrow sometime?"

"That's what I'm hoping."

"Here we go. Arnold...? Starts with a D?"

"Debs. Arn Debs."

"Right. Yeah, she just wants to check where and when."

"Would around eight be good? Here at the Mallard. In the Decoy Room?"

"You got it."

That evening, over dinner, I hardly said a word. And that night, after lights out, what happens but Tobe comes across...This is no impulse thing with Tobe. It's a task of major administration. Like the King Arthur movies—winching the knight up onto horseback. But it was all very gentle, all very sweet and dear, as I need it to be now. Now I'm sober. Before, I liked it to be rough, or I thought I did. These days I hate the idea of all that. Enough with the rough, I think. Enough rough.

• • •

The night train woke me around quarter of four. I lay there for a time with my eyes open. No chance of re-entry. So I got out of bed and made coffee and sat and smoked over my notes.

I'm upset. I'm upset anyway, but I'm also pissed about something personal. Here's what: The remarks and descriptions in Trader's letters. Why? They weren't unsympathetic. And I accept that I must have been a pretty pitiful sight back then—sweating it out behind drawn blinds. What am I concerned about? My privacy? Oh, sure. As I wind down from the job I begin to see these things more clearly. And *privacy* is what police spend their entire lives stomping on and riding roughshod over. Very, very soon you lose the whole concept of it. Privacy? Say what? No, what's bothering me, I think, is the stuff about my childhood. As if, given that, there could be no other outcome.

Here are two related things I have to set down.

First is the reason why I love Colonel Tom. Not the reason exactly, but the moment I knew it to be true. There was a high-profile murder up in the Ninety-Nine. A dead baby in a picnic cooler. Talk of drug wars and race riots. Media up the kazoo. I was passing his office and I heard him on the phone. Lieutenant Rockwell, as he then was, on the phone to the Mayor. And I heard him say, very deliberate: *My Mike Hoolihan is going to come and straighten this out.* I'd heard him use that parlance before. My Keith Booker.

My Oltan O'Boye. It was just the way he said it. "My Mike Hoolihan is going to come and straighten this out." I went into the toilet and bawled. Then I went and straightened out the murder in the Ninety-Nine.

The second thing is this. My father messed with me when I was a child. Out in Moon Park. Yeah he used to fuck me, okay? It started when I was seven and it stopped when I was ten. I made up my mind that after I hit double figures it just wasn't going to happen. To this end I grew the fingernails of my right hand. I sharpened them also, and hardened them with vinegar. This growing, this sharpening, this hardening: This was the reality of my resolve. On the morning after my birthday he came at me in my bedroom. And I almost ripped his fucking face off. I did. I had the fucking thing in my hand like a Halloween mask. I had it by the temple, just above the eye, and I sensed that with one more rip I could find out who my father really was. Then my mother woke up. We were never a model unit, the Hoolihans. By noon that same day we ceased to exist.

I'm what they call "state-raised." I was fostered some, but basically I'm state-raised. And as a child I always tried to love the state the way you'd love a parent, and I gave it a hundred percent. I've never wanted a kid. What I've wanted is a father. So how do we all stand, now that Colonel Tom doesn't have a daughter?

At 7:45 I called downtown. Johnny Mac: Mr. Whip on the midnights, which would now be falling apart. I asked him to have Silvera or whoever run a make on Arnold Debs.

I dug out my list: Stressors and Precipitants. Yeah, tell me about it. I crossed out 2 (Money?). And I crossed out 6 (*Deep* Secret? Trauma? Childhood?). This doesn't leave me with much.

Today I'm doing 3 (Job?). And tonight I'm doing Mr. Seven.

THE EIGHTY-BILLION-YEAR HEARTBEAT

Jennifer Rockwell, to say it all in one go, worked in the Department of Terrestrial Magnetism at the Institute of Physical Problems. The Institute lies well north of campus, in the foothills of Mount Lee, where the old observatory looms. What you do is: You take the MIE around CSU, skirting Lawnwood. And spend twenty minutes stuck in the Sutton Bay tailback. The Sutton Bay tailback: Another excellent reason for blowing your brains out.

Then you park the car and walk toward a low array of wood-clad buildings, expecting to be met by a forest ranger or a Boy Scout or a chipmunk. Here comes Chip. Here comes Dale. Here comes Woody Woodpecker, wearing a reversed baseball cap. The Department of Terrestrial Magnetism has the following words scrolled into the wall of its entrance corridor: ET GRITIS SICVT DEI SCIENTES BONVM ET MALVM. I got a translation from a kid who was passing: *And you will be like gods, knowing good and evil.* That's Genesis, isn't it? And isn't it what the Serpent says? Whenever I've been out to CSU—for a criminology lecture, an o.d., a student suicide around exam time—I've always had the same feeling. I think: It's a drag, not being young, but at least I don't have to take a test tomorrow morning. Another thing I notice, at the Institute of Physical Problems, is that someone has changed all the rules of attraction. Sexual allure is a physical problem that the students are no longer addressing. In my day, at the Academy, the women were all tits and ass and the men were all dick and bicep. Now the student body has no body. Now it's strictly sloppy-joe.

I am identified and greeted in the corridor by Jennifer's department head. His name is Bax Denziger and he's big in his discipline. He's big all right: Not a joint-splitter like my Tobe, but your regular bearish, bearded, flame-eyed, slobber-mouthed type with (you can bet) an inch-thick pelt all over his back. Yeah, one of those guys who's basically all bush. The little gap around the nose is the only clearing in the rain forest. He takes me into his office, where I feel I am surrounded by enormous quantities of information, all of it available, summonable, fingertip. He gives me coffee. I imagine asking permission to smoke, and imagine the way he'd say no: Totally relaxed about it. I repeat that I'm conducting an informal inquiry into Jennifer's death, prompted by Colonel and Mrs. Rockwell. Off the record—but is it okay if I use a tape recorder? Yes. He waves a hand in the air.

Bax Denziger, incidentally, is famous: TV-famous. I know stuff about him. He has a twin-prop airplane and a second home in Aspen. He is a skier and a mountaineer. He used to lift weights for the state. And I don't mean in prison. Three or four years ago he fronted a series on Channel 13 called "The Evolution of the Universe." And they have him on the news-magazine shows whenever something gives in his field. Bax here is a skilled "communicator" who talks in paragraphs as if to camera. And that's pretty much how I'm going to present it. The technical language should be right because I had Tobe run it by his computer.

I kicked off by asking him what Jennifer did all day. Would he please describe her work?

Certainly. In a department like ours you have three kinds of people. People in white coats who man the labs and the computers. People like Jennifer—postdocs, maybe assistant professors—who order the people in white coats around. And then people like yours truly. I order everyone around. Each day we have a ton of data coming in which has to be checked and processed. Which has to be *reduced*. That was Jennifer's job. She was also working on some leads herself. As of last fall she was working on the Milky Way's Virgo-infall velocity.

I asked him: Could you be more specific?

I am being specific. Perhaps I should be more general. Like everyone else here she was working on questions having to do with the age of the universe. A highly controversial and competitive field. A cutthroat field. We're looking at the rate of expansion of the universe, the rate of the deceleration of that expansion, and the total mass-density parameter. Respectively, in shorthand: Hubble's constant, q-nought, and dark matter. We're asking if the universe is open or closed...I look at you, Detective, and I see a resident of the naked-eye universe. I'm sure you don't bother too much with this stuff.

I said, well, no, I seem to make do okay without it. But please.

What we see out there, the stars, the galaxies, the galaxy clusters and superclusters, that's just the tip of the iceberg. That's just the snowcap on the mountain. At least 90 percent of the universe consists of dark matter, and we don't know what that dark matter is. Nor what it adds up to. If the total mass density is below a certain critical point, the universe will expand forever. The heavens will just go on getting emptier. If the total mass density is above a certain critical point, then gravity will eventually overcome expansion, and the universe will start to contract. From big bang to big crunch. Then— who knows?—big bang. And so on. What has been called the eighty-billion-year heartbeat.

I'm trying to give you an idea of the kinds of
things Jennifer thought about.

I asked him if Jennifer actually went up in the
telescope much. He smiled indulgently.

Bubble, bubble, Hoyle and Hubble. Allan
Sandage needs a bandage. Ah, the cage at
midnight, with your flask, your parka, your
leather ass and your iron bladder. The seeing! Detective—

Excuse me. The what?

The seeing. The seeing? Actually it's a
word we still use. The quality of the image.
Having to do with the clarity of the sky. The
truth is, Detective, we don't do much "seeing" anymore. It's all pixels and fiber optics
and CCDs. We're down at the business end of
it, with the computers.

I asked him the simple question. I asked him if
Jennifer was happy in her work.

I'll say! Jennifer Rockwell was an inspi-
ration to us all. She had terrific esprit. Persistent, tough, fair. Above all tough. In
every respect her intellect was tough.
Women…Let me rephrase this. Maybe not
at the Nobel level, but cosmology is a field
where women have made lasting contribu-

tions. Jennifer had a reasonable shot at adding to that.

I asked if she had an unorthodox side, a mystical side. I said, You guys are scientists, but some of you end up getting religion, right?

There's something in that. Knowing the mind of God, and so on. You're certainly affected by the incredible grandeur and complexity of revealed creation. But don't lose sight of the fact that it's *reality* we're investigating here. These things we're studying are very strange and very distant, but they're as real as the ground beneath your feet. The universe is everything religions are supposed to be, and then some, weird, beautiful, terrifying, but the universe *is the case*. Now, there are people around here who pride themselves on saying, "All this is just a physics problem. That's all." But Jennifer was more romantic than that. She was grander than that.

Romantic how?

She didn't feel marginalized, as some of us can do. She felt that this was a central human activity. And that her work was...pro bono. She felt that very strongly.

Excuse me? The study of stars is pro bono?

Now I'm going to speak with some freedom and optimism here. All set? In broad terms it makes sense to argue that the Renaissance and the Enlightenment were partly powered by the discoveries of Copernicus and Galileo. And Brahe and Kepler and others. You'd think that it would be desolating to learn that the earth was merely a satellite of the sun and that you'd lost your place at the center of the universe. But it wasn't. On the contrary. It was energizing, inspiring, liberating. It felt great to be in possession of a truth denied to each and every one of your ancestors. We don't act like we know it, but we're now on the edge of an equivalent paradigm shift. Or a whole series of them. The universe was still the size of your living room until the big telescopes came along. Now we have an idea of just how fragile and isolated our situation really is. And I believe, as Jennifer did, that when all this kicks in, this information that's only sixty or seventy years old, we'll have a very different view of our place and purpose here. And all this rat-race, turf-war, dog-eat-dog stuff we do all day will be revealed for what it is. The revolution is coming, Detective. And it's a revolution of consciousness. That's what Jennifer believed.

But you were fucking her, weren't you, Professor. And you wouldn't leave Betty-Jean.

I didn't actually say that last part. Though I kind of wanted to, by then. One of the things I knew about Bax Denziger: He's a twelve-kids-and-one-wife kind of guy. Still, for all his TV ease and brightness, and his high-saliva enthusiasm, I sensed uneasiness in him, reluctance—qualms. There was something he did and didn't want to reveal. And I too was in difficulty. I was having to relate his universe to mine. Having to, because Jennifer had linked them. And how *about* my universe, also real, also there, also *the case*, and with all its primitive passions. To him, my average day must look like psychotic soap opera—crazed surface activity. Jennifer Rockwell had moved from one world to the other, from revealed creation to the darkness of her bedroom. I pressed on, hoping that he and I, both, would find the necessary words.

Professor, were you surprised when you heard?

Consternated. We all were. Are. Consternated and devastated. Ask anybody here. The cleaning ladies. The Deans. That someone so...that someone of such radiance would choose to extinguish herself. I can't get my head around it. I really can't.

She ever get depressed that you knew of? Mood swings? Withdrawal?

No, she was unfailingly cheerful. She got frustrated sometimes. We all do. Because we—we're permanently on the brink of climax. We know so much. But there are holes in our knowledge bigger than the Bootes Void.

Which is?

It's more nothing than you could possibly imagine. It's a cavity 300 million light years deep. Where there's zip. The truth is, Detective, the truth is that human beings are not sufficiently evolved to understand the place they're living in. We're all retards. Einstein's a retard. I'm a retard. We live on a planet of retards.

Jennifer say that?

Yeah, but she also thought that that was what was so great about it. Beating your head against the lid.

She talked about death, didn't she. She talk to you about death?

No. Yes. Well not habitually. But we did have a discussion about death. Quite recently. It's been in my head. I've been playing it back. Like you do. I'm not sure if this thought was original to her. Probably not. But she put it...memorably. Newton, Isaac Newton, used to stare at the sun? He'd blind himself for days, for weeks, staring at the sun. Trying to figure the sun out. Jennifer— she was sitting right there where you're sitting. And she quoted some aphorism. Some French guy. Some duke. Went something like: "No man can stare at the sun or at death with a, with an unshielded eye." Now here's the interesting part. Do you know who Stephen Hawking is, Detective?

He's the...the guy in the wheelchair. Talks like a robot.

And do you know what a black hole is, Detective? Yeah, I think we all have some idea. Jennifer asked me: Why was it Hawking who cracked black holes? I mean, in the Sixties *everybody* was going at black holes hammer and tongs. But it was Stephen who gave us some answers. She said: Why him? And I gave the physicist's answer: Because he's the smartest guy around. But Jennifer wanted me to consider an explanation that was more—romantic. She said: Hawking understood black holes because he could *stare* at them. Black holes mean oblivion. Mean death. And Hawking has been staring at death all his adult life. Hawking could see.

Well, I thought: *That* isn't it. Just then Denziger looked at his watch with what seemed like irritation or anxiety. I said quickly,

"The revolution you talked about. Of consciousness. Would there be casualties?"

I heard the door open. A broad in a black sweatsuit was standing there, miming a phone call. When I turned again Denziger was still looking at me. He said,

"I guess it wouldn't necessarily be bloodless. I have to talk to Hawaii now."

"Yeah. Well I'm in no hurry. I'm going to smoke a

cigarette out on the steps there. Maybe if you get a moment you'll walk me to my car."

And I reached for the tape recorder and keyed the Pause.

With my arms folded to promote warmth and thought, I stood on the steps, looking at the quality of life. Jennifer's life. Jennifer's life. The fauna of early spring—birds, squirrels, even rabbits. And the agitated physicists—the little dweebs and nerds and wonks. A white sky giving way to pixels of blue, and containing both sun and moon, which she knew all about. Yes, and Trader, on the other side of the green hill. I could get used to this.

The naked-eye universe. The "seeing." The eighty-billion-year heartbeat. On the night she died, the sky was so clear, the seeing was so clear—but the naked eye isn't good enough and needs assistance...In her bedroom on the evening of March fourth Jennifer Rockwell conducted an experiment with time. She took fifty years and squeezed them into a few seconds. In moments of extreme crisis, time slows anyway: Calm chemicals come from the brain to the body, to help it through to the other side. How slowly time would have passed. She must have felt it. Jennifer must have felt it—the eighty-billion-year heartbeat.

Students straggled by. No, I don't have to take a test tomorrow morning. I'm done with being tested. Aren't I? Then why do I feel like I feel? Is Jennifer testing me? Is that what she's doing—setting me a test? The terrible thing inside of me is growing stronger. I swear to Christ, I almost feel pregnant. The terrible thing inside of me is alive and well, and growing stronger.

Blinking with his whole forehead, Bax Denziger staggered out into the light. He waved, approached— we fell into step. Without any prompting he said,

"I dreamt about you last night."

And I just said, "You did, huh?"

"I dreamt about this. And you know what I said? I said, 'Arrest me.' "

"Why would you say that, Bax?"

"Listen. The week before she died, for the first time ever Jennifer fucked up. She fucked up on the job. Big."

I waited.

He sighed and said, "I had her defending some distances in M101. Princeton were kicking our butt so bad—they were killing us. Let me keep it simple. The plate density scan gives you a bunch of numbers, millions of them, which go into the computer to be compared and calibrated against the algorithms. The—"

Stop, I said. The more you're telling me, the less I understand. Give me the upshot.

"She changed—she changed the program. I see the reductions on Monday morning and I'm like '*Yes.*' I'd been *praying* for data half that strong. I look again and I see it's all bullshit. The velocities, the metallicities—she'd changed all the values. And blown a month's work. I was up there nude against Princeton. Without a stitch on."

"Not an accident, you're saying. Not an honest mistake."

"No. It was like *malicious*. Get this. When Miriam phoned and told me, my first reaction was relief. Now I won't have to kill her when she comes in. And then just awful, awful guilt. Mike, it's been bleeding me white. I mean, am I that brutal? Did she fear my anger that much?"

By now we were in the lot and skirting around the unmarked. I'd fished my keys from my pants. Denziger looked as though mathematics were happening to him right then and there. As though math were happening to him: He looked subtracted, with much of his force of life, and his IQ, suddenly taken away.

"It's just a single element. In a pattern of egression," I said, looking to give him comfort with something that sounded technical. "You know Trader?"

"Sure I know him. Trader is a friend of mine."

"You tell him about Jennifer's stunt?"

"Stunt? No, not yet. But let me tell you something about Trader Faulkner. He's going to survive this. It'll take years, but he'll survive this. From what I gather it's uh, Tom Rockwell who has the biggest problem here. Trader's as strong as an ox but he's also a philosopher of science. He lives with unanswered questions. Tom's going to want something neat. Something that..."

"Measures up."

"Measures up." As I climbed into the car he gave a bushy frown and said, "That was a *good* joke she played on me. I keep getting into these professional brawls because my preferences are too strong. She always said I took the universe much too personally."

Tom's going to want something that measures up.
And again that thought: She was a cop's daughter. This
has to matter. How?

ARE YOU HERE TO MEET
JENNIFER ROCKWELL?

The Mallard is the best hotel in town, or it certainly
thinks it is. I know the Mallard well, because I've
always had a weakness (what's *wrong* with me?) for the
twenty-dollar cocktail. And for the twenty-cent cocktail, too. But I never resented the extra: It's worth it for
the atmosphere. A double Johnny Black in elegant sur-
roundings, with a sleepy-looking cocksucker, in a white
tux, slumped over the baby grand: That was my idea of
fun. Fortunately I never came in here when I was really
smashed. For a two-day climb, give me York's or Dree-
ley's on Division. Give me a long string of dives on Battery. The Mallard's the stone mansion in Orchard
Square. Inside it's all wooden panels and corporate
gloom. Recently refurbished. A high-tech shrine to
Great Britain. And with a lot of duck shit everywhere
you look. Prints, models, lures—decoys. Those little
carved quack-quacks, which have no value except rar-
ity, sell for tens of thousands. I got there early, equipped
with Silvera's literature on Arn Debs. I sat at a table and
ordered a Virgin Mary, heavy on the spice.

Arn Debs subscribes to *Business Week, Time,* and
Playboy. Naturally I'm thinking: Why did Jennifer give
him my number? Arn Debs drives a Trans Am and car-

ries a $7,000 limit on his MasterCard. Right now I
have to assume that she wanted me to cover or middle
for her—which I guess I would have gone ahead and
done. Arn Debs has season tickets to the Dallas Cow-
boys. Probably I'd cover for any woman on earth, in
principle—with one exception. Arn Debs rents action
movies by the shitload. With one exception: Jennifer's
mother. Arn Debs is a registered Republican. Nobody
seems to worry too much about Miriam: Maybe we
assume that, with her background, catastrophe is all
wired in. Arn Debs wears a bridge from eyetooth to
eyetooth. Here's another read: Jennifer gave him my
number because he was bothering her and she wanted
me to roust him. Arn Debs has three criminal convic-
tions. Two are for mail fraud: These are out of Texas.
One is for Aggravated Assault: This rap goes way
back—to when he was just an up-country boy.

Jennifer screwing up on the job: This could play
two ways. A rush of blood, maybe. Or a kind of personal inducement. Giving her one more reason not to
see Monday...

Now wait a minute. The Decoy Room was a zoo
when I walked in here. But eight o'clock has come and
gone. And I'm thinking, No: It's that fucking room-
emptier at the near end of the bar. How could I miss
the guy? I had him d.o.b.'d at 1/25/47. Six-three. Two
hundred and twenty. Red hair. I guess I just couldn't
feature it: Him and Jennifer, in any connection. And
I'd been watching him, too. There was no escaping Arn
Debs. Until around eight fifteen he was sticking to

beer—out of deference to his boner. Then he despaired and switched to scotch. Now he's swelling and swearing and sneering at the waitresses. And boring the barman blind: Asking the kid about his love life, his "prowess," as if it's the feminine of *prow.* Jesus, aren't drunks a drag? Barmen know all about bores and boredom. It's their job. They can't walk away.

I hang fire till the kid dreams up some chore for himself in back. Then I stride the length of the room. Everyone says I like to dress as a beat cop. As the beat cop I once was. But my jacket is black cotton, not black leather or sateen. And I wear black cotton pants, not the issue serge. And no nightstick, flashlight, radio, hat, gun. The man's wearing cowboy boots under his slacks. Another giant. Americans are going through the roof. Their mothers watch them grow, first with pride, then with panic.

"You Arn Debs?"

"Who the fuck wants to know?"

"The law," I said. "That's who the fuck wants to know." And I opened my jacket to show him the shield pinned to my blouse. "Are you here to meet Jennifer Rockwell?"

"Maybe and maybe not. And fuck you whichever."

"Yeah well she's *dead,*" I told him. And I made a quelling gesture with my raised palms. "Easy now, Mr. Debs. This is going to go just fine. We'll sit in the corner there and talk this thing through."

He said quietly, "Get your damn hand off of me."

And I said quietly, "Okay. You want to come and listen while I call the house? Do your wife and daughter know about Jennifer and you? Do they know about that spot of pain you had in August '81? With what's her face—September Duvall? That was a rape beef, wasn't it. Copped to Agg Assault. This was when you were still living up in Fuckbag, Nebraska. Remember?

"Eric?" I called to the barman. "Let me have a Virgin and a double Dewar's for the gentleman over at my table."

"Right away, Detective Hoolihan. Right away."

What I'm looking at here, I think (and he's sitting opposite me now, crowded into the nook by the window, with a hollow duck practically perched on each shoulder), is a semireformed shitkicker, in a good tweed coat and twills, who likes to get it wet at both ends whenever he's out of town. Table for two booked at the French restaurant upstairs. Tex tan, dark glasses ready in his top pocket, and a head of tawny hair he's real proud of—I'm surprised he's not called Randy or Rowdy or Red. High, wide, and handsome, with ittybitty eyes. A card-carrying tailchaser who's *that close* to being a fruit.

I said drink up, Mr. Debs.

He said well this is a hell of a turn for the evening to take.

I said so you're a friend of Jennifer Rockwell's.

He said yeah. Well. I only met her but once.

I said when?

He said oh, maybe a month back. I make these business trips regular, like every three or four weeks?

Met her on my last trip. February twenty-eight. I remember because no leap year. Met her February twenty-eight.

I said where?

He said here. Right here. At the bar there. She was sitting a couple of stools away and we got talking.

I said she was here alone. Not waiting for anybody.

He said yeah, sitting at the bar there with a white wine. You know.

I said so what were you thinking?

He said to tell you the truth, I thought she was like a model, or maybe even some kind of high-class call girl. Like you get in the better hotels. Not that I was fixing to pay for it. Then we got talking. I could tell she was a nice girl. She wasn't wearing a wedding band. She married?

I said what did you talk about?

He said life. You know. Life.

I said yeah? What? Sometimes you're up, sometimes you're down. Look before you leap. That kind of stuff?

He said hey. What is this? I'm answering your questions, okay?

I said you tell her about your wife and kid?

He said it didn't come up.

I said so you made a date. For tonight.

He said listen. I conducted myself like a gentleman.

Debs went into a thing about the company he works for in Dallas, how they had a guy come down from DC to give a seminar on social etiquette. A seminar on how to avoid sexual-harassment suits. He reminded me that you can't be too careful, not these days, and he always conducted himself like a gentleman.

I said what happened?

He said I said you feel like some dinner? Here at the hotel? She said I'd like that but tonight's a problem. Let's do it next time you're in town.

I said how come she gave you my phone number?

He said *your* phone number?

I said yeah. We talked yesterday.

He said that was *you*? Hey. Go figure. She said it wasn't *her* number. Said it was a friend's number. Said if I called her at home there might be a problem with the guy she lived with.

I said okay, swinger. That's not how it happened. Here's how it happened. You were hassling her. Wait! You were hassling her, in the bar, in the foyer, I don't know. Maybe you followed her out into the street. She gave you the number to get you off her back. You were—

He said that's not what happened. I swear. Okay, I escorted her out to the cab stand. And she wrote down the number for me. Look. Look.

From his inside pocket Debs produced his wallet. With his big fingers he leafed heavily through some loose business cards: There. He held it up for me. My number followed by Jennifer's crisp signature. Followed by two exes, crosses—for kisses.

I said you kiss her, Arn?

He said yeah I kissed her.

And he paused. It was gradually dawning on Debs that the momentum had turned his way. He was feeling good again now. What with the fomenting adrenaline, and the double Dewar's he'd long gotten down himself, as if against time.

"Yeah I kissed her. There a law against that now?"

"With your tongue, Arn?"

He straightened a finger at me. "I conducted myself with the upmost correctitude. Hey. Chivalry ain't dead. What she die of anyhow?"

Well that's something. *She's* dead. But chivalry isn't. "Accident. With a firearm."

"Hell of a thing. All that beauty. And the poise, you know?"

"Okay. Thanks, Mr. Debs."

"That's it?"

"Yeah. That's it."

He leaned closer. His breath, over and above the booze, was richly soured with male hormones. He said,

"We talked on the phone last night, I thought you were a guy. Not a little guy either. Somebody my size. People make mistakes. Right? I got real sure you were a woman when you showed me your shield. Give me another look at it. For your information, in my room I got a bottle of Krug in a ice bucket. Maybe tonight ain't a total wipe. Hey, what's the rush? You on duty? Come on. Stick around and have a real drink."

•　　•　　•

In the old days I would sometimes booze my way through clinical aversion. I used to take the pills that give you epileptic fits if you mix them with alcohol. And I'd mix them with alcohol. It felt like it was worth it. What the fuck. The convulsions only last for a few days. Then you don't have a problem.

I couldn't do that now. Mix me with alcohol, and the result would be fulminant hepatic failure. I couldn't drink my way through *that* shit. Because I wouldn't be around.

It's not too late. I'm going to change my name. To something feminine. Like Detective Jennifer Hoolihan.

For a girl to have a boy's name, and to keep it— that's not so unusual. I've come across a Dave and a Paul who never tried to pretty things up with Davina or Pauline. I've even met another Mike. We stuck with it. But how many grown men do I know who are still called Priscilla?

Here's something I've often wondered: Why did my father call me Mike if he was going to fuck me? Was he a fruit, too, on top of everything else? Here's something even more mysterious: I never stopped loving my father. I have never stopped loving my father. Whenever I think of him, before I can do anything about it, I feel great love flooding my heart.

And here comes the night train. First, the sound of knives being sharpened. Then its cry, harsh but symphonic, like a chord of car horns.

ALL HOLE

The dispatcher directs you to a large Tudor-style residence on Stanton Hill. Two tearful parents, supported by a small cast of tearful servants, lead you up the staircase. With your partner at your side (Silvera, in this case), you enter a bedroom infested with stereo and computer equipment, with CDs and PCs, with posters of babes and rock stars all over the walls, and on the bed is the corpse of some poor kid with a weak leer and an earring. His pants are down around his hightops. He is lying in a pool of skin magazines and amyl nitrate. There is also a rented adult video in the VCR and, beside the pillow, a remote smothered in latents. And he has a polyethylene bag half wrenched off his face. So you spend an hour with the folks, saying what you can, while the science crew come and go. And as soon as you're back in the unmarked, you both give the cop shrug and one of you will start:

Well at least he died in a good cause.

Right. He didn't give it up lightly. And you know what else?

What?

He was doing it for all of us.

He had no thought for himself up there.

He was pushing out the boundaries for all of us.

Laying his life on the line for all of us.

Greater love hath no man.

Than him who.

Lays down his life.

For a better handjob.

Well put. For a better handjob.

With TV you expect everything to measure up. Things are meant to measure up. The punishment will answer the crime. The crime will fall within the psychological profile of the malefactor. The alibi will disintegrate. The gun will smoke. The veiled woman will suddenly appear in the courthouse.

Motive, motive. "Motive": That which moves, that which impels. But with homicide, now, we don't care about motive. We never give it a second's thought. We don't care about the why. We say: Fuck the why. Motive might have been worth considering, might have been pretty reliable, might have been in okay shape half a century ago. But now it's all up in the fucking air. With the TV.

I'll tell you who wants a why. *Jurors* want a why. They want reruns of *Perry Mason* and *The Defenders*. They want *Car Fifty-Four, Where Are You?*

They want commercials every ten minutes or it never happened.

That's homicide. This is suicide. And we all want a why for suicide.

And how's it looking?

Tomorrow night I'm seeing Trader Faulkner, and something new, something more, may emerge from that. But otherwise it's pretty much made. It's down. Isn't it? I have followed up all the names in Jennifer's address book. I have been through the phone records and the credit-card accounts. And there's only one gap:

No hit on the lithium. Tony Silvera has been onto Adrian Drago in Narcotics, and they gave their snitches a roust. But this isn't a street drug we're talking about. And I don't build on nailing the connect.

But—hey. Jennifer Rockwell was a cleavage in a lab coat. But she wasn't Mary Poppins. A spinning top looks still and stable until the force starts to weaken. A tremor, then it slows and slews. It wobbles and reels and clatters. Then it stops.

Answers are coming together, are they not? We got sex and drugs and rock and roll. This is more than you usually get. This is plenty. This is practically TV.

So why don't I buy it?

I keep thinking about her body. I keep thinking about Jennifer's body and the confidence she had in it. See her in a swimsuit and you just thought...One summer day five or six years ago the Rockwells took the whole roof pool at the Trum, for their anniversary, and when Jennifer came out of the cabana and walked toward us in her white one-piece we all fell silent for a beat, and Silvera said, "Hm. Not bad." Then Grandma Rebka clapped her hands together and wailed, "*Zugts afen mir!*" It should be said about me. We should all be so lucky. The sight of her instantly had you going along with the idea that the basis of attraction is *genetic*. Get Jennifer, and your genes would surge forth, in a limo. Her body was kind of an embarrassment, a thrilling embarrassment, to everyone (even Trader dipped his head). But it wasn't an embarrassment to her. The confidence with which she carried it was self-evident, self-sufficient—I guess the word I want is "consummate." She never needed to give it a moment's thought. And when you consider how much the rest of us think about our bodies, and what kind of thoughts these are. Yes, absolutely right. We should all be so lucky.

Something else was said that day, around the roof pool at the Trum. The two grandmas, Rebka and Rhiannon, who died within a month of each other the following year—they were a great double act. As a ten-year-old Rebka had cleaned the streets of Vienna with her father's skullcap. And she was an angel of light. Silver-spoon Rhiannon, on the other hand, was dour, sarcastic, and mean. And Welsh. If you thought *Schadenfreude* was a German word, then five minutes with Rhiannon would make you think again. And the mouth on her, still with that accent. She could even shock me. In a long life of uninterrupted ease, Grandma Rhiannon had one real cause for complaint. All her children grew and flourished. But she'd had fifteen of them.

Out by the pool, that day, she said,

"I'm like a horse in the bullring. I've got bags of sawdust in me."

And I said, "Is that a Welsh thing? I thought it was an Irish thing, having a ton of kids."

"No, not reely. It was him. Billy. It was him wanted them. I only wanted two. Even after little Alan he was on at me to have more."

"More?"

"Day and night. Just one more. I'd say, 'Come on, Billy. Give it a rest. I'm awl awl as it is.' "

"You're what?"

She pronounced the two words the same. Awl awl. All hole.

That's what I sometimes think this case is.

All hole.

CHANGING ALL THE GIVENS

Tonight's my date with Trader.

One thing I do, before I go over there, is dig out the transcript of the interrogation I conducted downtown. My effort, there in the small interrogation room, was misdirected. But I'm impressed by its tenacity. Now I see this:

> I have a witness that puts you outside the
> house at seven thirty-five. Looking distressed.
> "Mad." Riled-up. Sound familiar, Trader?
> Yes. The time. And the mood.

I missed that earlier, and I now remind myself to pick up on it tonight. Why distressed?

Another thing I do, before I leave, is spend about an hour in the bathroom with the concealer. And the contour powder and the lip-liner. And the tweezers for Christ's sake. Too, I'd washed my hair the night before, and had an early one. I guess a person will sometimes do this, no real reason attaching except for herself, to feel at her best around a man she likes. Another explanation may be that I have a crush on Trader. Well? So? It doesn't mean anything. Say only this: If he wants comfort, I will give it to him. On my way out the door Tobe looked at me oddly. Tobe's okay. He's a gentle giant. As opposed to a violent one. As opposed to Deniss, Shawn, Jon, Duwain.

Long ago I learned that I cannot get the good guys.

I am one of the good guys, and I go out there and get the bad guys. I can get the bad guys.

But I cannot get the good guys.

I just cannot get the good guys.

It was a long evening, and it went in drifts.

Trader has moved back into the apartment. My death scene has been destroyed: It's been redecorated. The chair in the bedroom—the same chair?—sits swathed in a white sheet. A stepladder still stands in the corner. Trader says he hasn't yet slept in there. He ends up on the couch. Watching TV.

"Hey. A TV. You got a life at last," I said. Innocent words were proving difficult to find. "What's it like, being here?"

"It's better being here than not being here."

Again: Taken generally, this was not an opinion that Jennifer Rockwell would have shared.

I stood around in the kitchen while he fixed me a soda. Ice and lemon. Trader's body was always slow-moving. This night his face, too, seemed to bear the shadow of ponderousness. If it wasn't for the math and everything, at odd moments you might almost have figured him for one of those morons in a matinee mask—one of those guys given good looks for no good reason. Except to spread a little more grief. But then the light of intelligence would return to the brown softness of his eyes. I tried to remember if he'd always had this frown, this shadow. Or did he pick it up a month ago, on March fourth? The birthdate of so much stupefaction. He was drinking. He drank steadily all evening. Jack Daniel's. Rocks.

Raising his glass, he turned to me and said, "Well, Mike?"

But he never turned to me and said, *What have you got? What did you learn?* I wanted to know what he knew. He didn't want to know what I knew.

At times, our talk was very—what shall I say?— orderly:

How about children, Trader? I guess I'm still looking for a precipitant that's the right shape and size. Might she have had anxiety about that?

There was no pressure on her. I was pretty keen but I'd never push it. If she wanted none—fine. If she wanted ten—also fine. It's like abortion. It's the woman's call.

This is left-field: How did she feel about abortion?

It was about the only agenda-type issue she was interested in. Libertarian, but with great qualms. Me too. That's why I goof off on the subject and hand it over to the women.

· · ·

At times, not so orderly. At times, our talk tended toward the not so orderly:

"Look at this."

He was in the armchair, his reading chair, next to a round table on which books were stacked—also lamp, glass, framed photographs. Now he reached for a certain ruffled paperback, saying,

"It was in the shelves with its spine to the wall. I can't believe she actually read it."

"Why's that?"

"It's so lousily written."

A small-press publication, called *Making Sense of Suicide*. By some doctor with two middle initials. I flicked through it. Not one of those how-to guides that have recently been getting a lot of play. Written more from the counseling end of the operation—crisis center, help-line, talk-down.

"She made marks," I said.

"Yeah. Habit. She always read with a pencil in her hand. I don't know when she bought it. Could have been anytime in the last ten years."

"She signed it."

"But she didn't date it. And her signature—her handwriting settled down pretty early. Why don't you nuke it, Mike? With your forensic arsenal. The boron-activation test. Wasn't that it?"

I sat back. I couldn't quite get a take on his mood. I said, "That was Colonel Tom, Trader. The guy was down to his last marble. I had to do it for Tom."

"Hey, I got one for you. Tom did it."

"Did what?"

"Killed Jennifer. Murdered Jennifer."

"Come again?"

"He's the least likely guy. So it has to be him. Come on, we can cook this shit up. All you need is a little irresponsibility. It's like redecorating the bedroom—you can do it a hundred ways. Miriam did it. Bax Denziger did it. *You* did it. But let's stick with Tom. Tom did it. He waits till I leave. Then he sneaks in and does it."

"Okay. Then why doesn't he let it sleep? Why'd he crank *me* up? What am I doing sitting here tonight?"

"That's a blind. That's just a diversion. So the truth would never occur to anyone sane."

"Motive?"

"Easy. I got it. Jennifer recalled a terrible secret from her past. A memory she tried to suppress. With drugs."

"With drugs?"

"When she was just a little girl, she asked her daddy...why he came to her bedroom. Why he made her do those bad things. Why he...Oh no. Oh. I'm sorry, Mike."

"That's okay. But let's stop this. Jennifer did it."

"Jennifer did it. See? Why doesn't everyone just keep their mouth shut. Why doesn't everyone...just shut the fuck up."

Then a revelation:

Did you talk to Professor Denziger?

Yeah I talked to Bax.

He told you what—

Yeah, he did. He agonized good about that. I thought it was kind of typical of her in a way. Not the incompetence. That wasn't typical. But how she did it. Changing the values. Changing all the givens.

Why's that?

Like if you said to her, I don't know, who's going to win the election in November, she had trouble getting interested. Because of the givens. The parameters. Not just the candidates—the whole thing. For her the thread had gotten lost so long ago.

Did Denziger tell you that what she did looked deliberate?

I think the only way you can genuinely go wrong there is when you have an ax to grind. Like when Sandage started wowing everyone with his quasar discoveries. His results were contaminated by brown dwarves, which quasars can resemble. It's like in tennis: You want the ball to be good so much you actually *see* it good when it's not. Jennifer wouldn't see anything that wasn't there. I think it was just part of the pattern.

You said she wasn't the pattern type.

But that's what mental illness does—it ropes you into a pattern. Some very corny stuff. There's something else she did too. She started *buying* things.

What? Don't tell me. Cars. Pianos.

No, paintings. Real crap, too. She wasn't particularly visual, and I'm not either. But they look like airport art to me. I keep turning deliveries away. The galleries don't holler. It's a suicide. They've seen this before.

She used post-dated checks.

...Yeah. Post-dated checks. There were two deliveries on Friday. The checks were dated April first.

April Fool.

April Fool.

Then another revelation:

He'd just bummed a smoke off me: His first of the evening. I was halfway through my second pack. I said,

"This might surprise you, but I don't think so. From the autopsy. Toxicology? I get the feeling Tom's told you about it."

"Miriam told me about it. She tells me everything in the end. The lithium? I played dumb. But I already knew."

"You knew Jennifer was on lithium?"

"Not while she was alive I didn't." He sighed and said, "Mike, tell me something. That book... *Making Sense of Suicide* doesn't make sense of suicide, or anything else. But it's extra vague on suicide notes. How many suicides leave suicide notes?"

That's a very slippery stat, and I told him so.

"And what's the difference? What does it mean?"

Nothing in itself, I said. Depends on the person, depends on the note. Some offer comfort. Others, blame.

"She left a note. She left a note. She sent me a note by U.S. Mail. I went back to the office a week later and it was there in my tray. Here, help yourself. Now

I'm going to do what she did on Saturday morning, when she posted it. I'm going to take a walk around the block."

I waited till I heard the door. I huddled down over the tape recorder. I tried to raise my voice above a whisper—and I couldn't. I had to use the volume control on the machine, because mine just wasn't working.

"My darling," I whispered. "You're back at work now and that consoles me. That, and the fact that you're the kindest lover on the planet and will eventually have to forgive me for what I've done.

"You knew me ten times better than anyone, but I wasn't quite what you thought I was. Almost exactly a year ago I started getting the sense that I was losing control of my thoughts. That's the only way I can put it. My thoughts went about their thought thing, doing what they had to do, while I was just an innocent bystander. I didn't dare go through Tulkinghorn, because I couldn't trust him not to run to Dad. I thought I could fix it myself—which might have been part of the internal liar dice. I read up on it. And when you thought I was at the Brogan on Mondays I was at Rainbow Plaza where all the GCG people take their lunchbreaks on the lawn. You never scored a dime-bag so easy. Since last May I've been on varying doses of a stabilizer. Serzone, depecote, tegretol—they sound like moral stances. They dry your head out. But they stopped helping.

"I'm frightened. I keep thinking I'm going to do something that nobody's ever done before—something

altogether inhuman. Is that what I'm doing now?
Baby, I'm staying with you until tomorrow night. You
were perfect for me. And remember that you couldn't
have done *anything any different.*

"Help Ma. Help Dad. Help Dad. I'm sorry I'm
sorry I'm sorry I'm sorry I'm sorry I'm sorry I'm sorry
I'm sorry I'm sorry..."

And so it went on, over the page to the end of the
sheet: I'm sorry.

Some time later I was in the kitchen again, drinking
soda again. Watching the man move around again.
Not just the cold air had pushed the blood into his
cheeks. His movements, now, were sharper and noisier, tinnier. And his breath sounded raw. I changed the
tape. I smoked. Feeding the thing inside of me. The
thing inside of me—it wasn't any calmer. It too was
sharper, noisier—colder, angrier.

He said over his shoulder: "Mike, don't you have
symptoms when you're on that shit? Physical symptoms?"

"Yeah, you can do," I said.

"Doesn't your face swell up and your hair fall out?"

"It can do, yeah. Suddenly you're Kojak."

"Mike, you'll believe me when I say...My faith in
my powers of observation have—has seen better days.
I lived with a mood-drugged suicide for a year without
noticing. Maybe I wouldn't even have noticed that I
was living with Kojak. But I'd have noticed that I was
fucking him, wouldn't I? Reassure me."

"Some people don't get any physical symptoms. Not double vision. Not even the breath. Jennifer. Jennifer was very lucky with her body."

"A *pity* about that. A *pity* about that."

Her shine is leaving these rooms. Jennifer's will to order is leaving these rooms. Slow male entropy is beginning—but for the time being nothing else has changed. Her blue trunk still occupies its place beneath the window. Her bureau lies open in its ante-mortem busyness. The bowl of potpourri goes on aging between the lamp and the framed photograph on the table we're sitting at.

"Jesus," I said, smiling, "what was she on? Magic mushrooms?"

Trader leaned forward. "Jennifer?"

Graduation: In the photograph the three girls are standing—no, bending—in their robes and flat hats. Jennifer is laughing with her mouth about as wide as a mouth can go. Her eyes are moist seams. The two friends don't appear to be in much better shape. But there is the fourth girl in the photograph, trapped in the corner of the frame, and she seems immune to this laughter—immune, maybe, to any laughter at all.

"No," he said. "Jennifer? No. See, this is where it stops adding up for me."

He paused—and then came the frown or the shadow.

"What does?" I said. "What stops?"

"She *hated* anything mood-altering—for herself. I mean, she did the usual shit at college like everybody else. But then she quit and that was that. You know Jennifer. One glass of wine, but never two. She had a thing about it. The whole first year I met her, she had this crazy housemate who was—"

"Phyllida," I said. And saw that shadow again.

"Phyllida. She was taking zinc and manganese and steel and chrome. And Jennifer said, 'She's eating a Sherman tank every day. What do you expect? She isn't *anyone* now.' I mean, I like to drink some nights and I like to smoke a little weed, and Jennifer never had a problem with that. But for herself? No sleeping pills, nothing. Even an aspirin was a last resort."

"She keep up with this Phyllida?"

"No, thank God. A few letters. She got farmed out to her stepmother. And they moved to Canada. That *was* a buzz."

After a time I said, "You mind if I ask you a personal question?"

"Come on, Mike. Don't be ridiculous."

How was your sex life?

Good, thanks.

I mean in the last year. You didn't feel that it was dropping off a little?

Maybe. It might have dropped off a little, I guess.

Because that's almost always a sign. So how often were you making love?

Oh, I don't know. I suppose in the last year it was down to once or twice a day.

A day? You don't mean once or twice a week?

Once or twice a day. But more at the weekend.

And who would initiate?

Huh?

Was it always your idea? Listen. Tell me to fuck off and everything, but some women, when they're *that* good-looking, it's like honey from the icebox. It won't spread. What was she like in the sack?

...Adorable. Relax. I'm feeling good telling you this. It's funny. That letter you saw is about the only one she ever sent me that's halfway printable. She used to say, "Do you think anyone would *believe* how much of our time we spend doing this? Two rational adults?" When we went south on vacation, we'd come back and everyone would ask us why we didn't have a tan.

So sex was a big part of it.

It didn't come in parts.

...You never sensed any restlessness in her? I mean, she hooked up with you pretty early. You don't think she might have felt she'd missed out?

Well, what the fuck do I know. Listen, Mike, what can I tell you. Let me say how it was with us. We never really wanted to be with anybody else. It was kind of worrying. We had friends, we had brothers, and we saw a lot of Tom and Miriam, and we went to parties and hung with our crowd. But we never liked that as much as we liked being with each other. We spent our time talking, laughing, fucking and working. Our idea

of a night out was a night in. Are you telling me people don't want that? We kept expecting it to quieten
down but it never did. I didn't own her. I wasn't secure
in her a hundred percent—because once you are, the
best is over. I knew there was a part of her I couldn't
see. A part she kept for herself. But it was a part of her
intellect. It wasn't some fucking *mood*. And I think she
felt the same about me. We felt the same about each
other. Isn't that what we're all meant to want?

I was a long time leaving. Already I had my bag on my
lap when I said,

"The letter. You have that in your wallet when I
yanked you downtown?" He nodded. I said, "That
might have taken some of the wind out of my sails."

"Mike, you didn't have any wind in your sails. You
just thought you did."

"I had Colonel Tom, is what I had. It might have
speeded things up."

"Yeah, but I didn't want things speeded up. I
wanted them slowed down."

"On March fourth. You said she seemed cheerful.
All day. 'Typically cheerful.' "

"That's right. Ah but see, Jennifer thought you
had a moral duty to be cheerful. Not to seem cheerful.
To be cheerful."

"And you, dear? You said that, as you were leaving, you felt 'distressed.' Why 'distressed'?"

His face was blank. But then a look of hilarious

humiliation moved quickly across it. He closed his eyes and leaned his head on his hand.

"Another time." And he stood up, saying, "Let's do 'distressed' another time."

We were in the hall and he was helping me on with my jacket. And he touched me. He lifted the hair out from under my collar, and smoothed his hand across my spine. I felt confusion. I turned and said,

"When people do this...When people do what she did, there's a thing that makes it different. They end it, they get out. It's over for them. But they kind of flip it over to you."

He considered me closely for a second. He said, "No, I haven't found that."

"You okay, honey?"

I gave him my softest look. But I was daunted, I think. Could I honestly say that Jennifer was an act I could even take his mind off, let alone follow? And if you aren't digging yourself, at such moments, then nobody else is going to dig you. And maybe my look wasn't so soft. Maybe, now, my softest look just isn't so soft.

"Yeah. You okay, Mike? This place," he said, and he glanced around vaguely. "I realize...Have you ever lived with somebody who was physically beautiful? Physically."

"No," I said, without having to think. Without having to think of Deniss, of Duwain, of Shawn, of Jon.

"I realize now what an incredible luxury that was. This place—I guess this place is still pretty nice. But now it feels like a flop to me. Like a dump. Cold-water. Walk-up."

All I came home with, then, was *Making Sense of Suicide.*

And in its pages, against all expectation (it is, as Trader said, lousily written, as well as smug and sanctimonious and seriously out-of-date), I would find what I needed to know.

The trail was cold, the trail was at absolute zero. But then I shivered—the way you do when you finally start to get warm.

NOW THERE'S NOTHING

I got back to the apartment around midnight.

In the bedroom I stood over Tobe for the longest time. What *he* goes through with his body. It's all he can do just to sit there on a summer evening, watching a game show, with a beer can sweating into his hand. Even in sleep he suffers. Like a mountain is always in pain. The slipping discs of its tectonic plates. The gristle caught between crust and mantle.

When I quit working murders and had nothing much before me all day except the slow work of keeping dry, I used to stay up until the night train came— whenever. And then the long sleep. Until the night train came. Causing panic among the crockery. Shaking the ground beneath my feet.

And that's what I intend to do now. Until whenever.

•   •   •

*My Mike Hoolihan is going to come and straighten this
out.*

I did go. And I did straighten out the killing in the
Ninety-Nine.

It was a totally God-awful murder—I mean, for
hunger—but it was the kind of case that homicide
cops have sex dreams about: Basically, a newsworthy
piece of shit with frills. Basically, a politically urgent,
headline-hogging dunker. Quickly solved by concen-
tration and instinct.

The body of a fifteen-month-old baby boy had
been found in a picnic cooler in a public recreation
facility in the Ninety-Nine, over to Oxville. A precinct
canvass had brought investigators to a rowhouse on
the 1200 block of McLellan. By the time I showed there
was a cordoned crowd of maybe a thousand people lin-
ing the street, a gridlock of media trucks, and, up
above, a Vietnam of geostationary network helicopters.

Inside, five detectives, two squad supervisors and
the Dep Comm were wondering how to get this show
downtown without a prime-time riot. Meanwhile they
were questioning a twenty-eight-year-old female,
LaDonna, and her boyfriend, DeLeon. A decade ago, a
month ago, in recounting this, I would have said that
she was a PR and he was a Jake. Which is true. But
suffice it to say that they were people of color. Also
present, sitting on kitchen chairs and swinging their
white-socked feet, were two silent little girls of thirteen
and fourteen, Sophie and Nancy—LaDonna's kid sis-

ters. LaDonna also maintained that it was her baby and her Igloo.

It's kind of an average Oxville scenario: The family is enjoying a picnic (this is January), the toddler wanders off (wearing only a diaper), they start searching for him (in this open field), and are unsuccessful (and go home). Forgetting the Igloo. According to LaDonna, the explanation stares you in the face. The toddler eventually returned and climbed into the picnic cooler and pulled the lid down (engaging the external catch) and suffocated. Whereas the ME's initial finding, soon to be confirmed by autopsy, is that the child died of strangulation. According to DeLeon, things are a little more complicated. As they were leaving the recreational facility, their search abandoned, they saw a gang of white skinheads—known nazis and drugdealers—climb out of a truck and head for that part of the open field where the child was last seen.

We're all sitting there, listening to these two brain surgeons, but I'm watching the girls. I'm watching Sophie and Nancy. And the whole thing went transparent. This was all it took: From the adjoining bedroom came the sound of a baby's cry. A baby waking, dirty or hungry or lonely. LaDonna kept talking—she never skipped a beat—but Sophie rose an inch from her seat for a second, and Nancy's face suddenly swelled with hatred. Immediately I saw:

LaDonna was not the mother of the murdered boy. She was his grandmother.

Sophie and Nancy were not LaDonna's kid sisters. They were her daughters.

Sophie was the mother of the waking baby in the bedroom. Nancy was the mother of the baby in the Igloo.

Sophie was the murderess.

It was down. We even got a motive: Earlier the same day, Nancy had taken Sophie's last diaper.

I was on the six o'clock news that night, nationwide.

"This murder was not about race," I reassured 150 million viewers. "This murder was not about drugs." Everyone can relax. "This murder was about a diaper."

There are three things I didn't tell Trader Faulkner.

I didn't tell Trader that, in my view, Jennifer's letter was not the work of a woman under terminal stress. I've seen a hundred suicide notes. They have things in common. They express insecurity—and they are barren, arid. "Serzone, depecote, tegretol—they sound like moral stances." Toward the finish of the lives of suicides, more or less all their thoughts are self-lacerating. Whether they soothe or snarl, cringe or strut, suicide notes do not seek to entertain.

I didn't tell Trader that with an affective, or emotional, disorder the sexual drive sharply declines. Nor did I add that with an ideational, or organic, disorder it almost invariably disappears. Unless the mania is itself sexual. Which gets noticed.

I didn't tell Trader about Arn Debs. Not just because I didn't have the heart. But because I never believed in Arn Debs. I didn't believe in Arn Debs for a single second.

Time 1:45.

Random thoughts:

Homicide can't change—and I don't mean the department. It can evolve. It can't change. There's nowhere for homicide to go.

But what if suicide could change?

Murder can evolve in the direction of increasing disparity—new *dis* murders.

Upward disparity:

Sometime in the Fifties a man made a homicidal breakthrough. He planted and detonated a bomb on a commercial airliner: To kill his wife.

A man could bring down—perhaps has brought down—a 747: To kill his wife.

The terrorist razes a city with a suitcase H-bomb: To kill his wife.

The President entrains central thermonuclear war: To kill his wife.

Downward disparity:

Every cop in America is familiar with the super-savagery of Christmas Day domestics. On Christmas Day, everyone's home at the same time. And it's a disaster...We call them "star or fairy?" murders: People get to arguing about what goes on top of the tree. Here's another regular: Fatal stabbings over how you carve the bird.

A murder about a diaper.

Imagine: A murder about a safety-pin.

A murder about a molecule of rancid milk.

But people have already murdered for less than that. Downward disparity has already been plumbed— been sonar-ed and scoured. People have already murdered for nothing. They take the trouble to cross the street to murder for nothing.

Then there's copycat, where the guy's copying the TV or some other guy, or copying some other guy who's copying the TV. I believe that copycat is as old as Homer, older, older than the first story daubed in shit on the wall of the cave. It precedes the fireside yarn. It precedes fire.

You get copycat with suicide too. Fuck yes. They call it the Werther Effect. Named after a melancholy novel, later suppressed after it burned a trail of youth suicides through eighteenth-century Europe. I see the same thing here on the street: Some asshole of a bass guitarist chokes on his own ralph (or fries on his own amplifier)—and suddenly suicide is all over town.

There's a recurring anxiety, with every generation, that a *shoah* of suicides has come, to blow the young away. It seems like everybody's doing it. And then it settles down again. Copycat is more precipitant than cause. It just gives shape to something that was going to happen anyway.

Suicide hasn't changed. But what if it *did* change? Homicide has dispensed with the why. You have gratuitous homicide. But you don't—

•   •   •

It's 2:30 and the phone is ringing. I suppose that for a regular person this would mean drama, or even catastrophe. But I picked it up as if it was ringing in the P.M.

"What?"

"Mike. Are you still up? I got another one for you."

"Yes, Trader, I'm still up. Are we going to do 'distressed' now?"

"Consider this a preamble to 'distressed.' I got one for you. Are you ready?"

His voice wasn't slurred—it was slowed: Idling at around 33 rpm.

"Wait a second. I'm ready."

There's a widowed mailman who has worked all his life in a small town. A small town with extreme weather conditions. Retirement is nearing. One night he sits up late. Composing an emotional farewell to the community. Stuff like: "I have served you in ice and in rain, in the thunder and the sunshine, under lightning, under rainbows..." He has it printed up. And on his last but one day he drops a copy into every mailbox on his run.

The next morning is bleak and cold. But the response to his letter is warm enough. He has a cup of coffee here, a slice of hot pie there. He waves away the modest cash gifts he's offered. He shakes hands, he moves on. A little disappointed, maybe, that no one seems to have been stirred by the—by the quality of his dedication. By its poetry, Mike.

Last stop on his round is the house of a retired Hollywood lawyer and his nineteen-year-old wife. She's a retired hatcheck girl. Gorgeous. Full-figured. Wide-eyed. He rings the bell and she answers. "You're the man who wrote the letter. About the thunder and the sunshine? Come in, sir, please."

In the dining room there's a table groaning with exotic food and wine. She says her husband has just left for Florida on a golfing trip. Would he care to stay for lunch? After coffee and liqueurs she leads him by the hand to the white fur rug in front of the glowing fire. They make love for three hours. In the amber light, Mike. He can't believe the intensity of it. The strength of it. Was it that very poetry that had so moved the young woman? Was it the rainbows? He thinks that, at the very least, she's his for life.

He gets dressed in a daze. Wearing a flimsy housecoat, she leads him to the front door. Then she reaches for her purse on the hall table. She offers him a five-dollar bill.

And he says, "What's this for? I'm sorry, I don't understand."

And she says, "Yesterday morning, over breakfast, I read your letter out loud to my husband? About the ice and the rain and the

lightning? I said, 'What the hell am I supposed to do about this guy?' He said, 'Fuck
him, give him five bucks.' And lunch was my
idea."

I managed a kind of laugh.

"You don't get it."

"No, I get it. She did love you, Trader. I'm sure of
that."

"Yeah, but not enough to stick around. Okay. Let's
do 'distressed.' I apologize in advance. It'll be no damn
use to you."

"Let's do it anyway."

"We spent Sunday nights apart. So it always
seemed like a good idea to go to bed together late Sunday afternoon. That's what we always did. And that's
what we did on March fourth. I'd like to say, I'd really
like to say it felt different, that Sunday. Like during the
act of love she 'went away,' or 'disappeared.' Or some
such. We could cook something up, couldn't we? Have
her say something like, 'Don't make me pregnant.' But
no. It was exactly like it always was. I drank a beer. I
said goodbye. So why was I 'distressed'?"

By now his voice was sounding like my tape
recorder when the battery's about to fritz. I lit a cigarette and waited.

"Okay. On my way down the stairs, I tripped on
my shoelace. I knelt to retie it, and it snapped. I also
caught a hangnail in my sock. On my way out the side
door I ripped my coat pocket on the handle. That's it.

So when I hit the street I was naturally very 'distressed.' Mike, I was suicidal."

I wanted to say: I'll come over.

" 'Fuck him, give him five bucks.' I thought that was pretty funny the first time around. Now it makes me scream with laughter."

I wanted to say: I'm coming over.

"Oh, Christ. I just didn't get it, Mike."

That list headed Stressors and Precipitants—there's not much left of it now. To keep myself quietly amused, I think about compiling another list, one that would go something like:

Astrophysics	Asset Forfeiture
Trader	Tobe
Colonel Tom	Pop
Beautiful	

But where's the point in that? *Zugts afen mir,* right? We should all be so lucky. And even though we aren't, we're still here.

Stressors and Precipitants. What remains? We have: 7. Other *Significant Other?* And we have: 5. *Mental Health? Nature of disorder: a) psychological? b) ideational/organic? c) metaphysical?*

Now I cross out 7. I cross out Arn Debs.

Now I cross out 5 a). After some thought I cross

out 5 c). And then my head gives a sudden nod and I cross out 5 b). That, too, I excise.

Now there's nothing.

It's 3:25 before it hits me. Yesterday was Sunday. The night train must have been through hours ago. Hours ago, the night train came and went.

On the evening Jennifer Rockwell died, the sky was clear and the visibility excellent.

But the seeing—the seeing, the seeing—was no good at all.

PART THREE

THE SEEING

This is where I felt it first: In the armpits. On March fourth Jennifer Rockwell fell burning out of a clear blue sky. And that's where I first felt the flames. In my armpits.

I woke late. And alone—though not quite. Tobe was long gone. But somebody else was just leaving.

The morning after she died Jennifer was in my room. Standing at the foot of the bed till I opened my eyes. Then of course she disappeared. She returned the next day: Fainter. And again, and always fainter. But this morning she was back with all her original power. Is that why the parents of dead children spend half the rest of their lives in darkened rooms? Are they hoping the ghosts will return with all their original power?

She wasn't just standing there, this time. She was pacing, for hours, pacing swiftly, bent, lurching. I felt that Jennifer's ghost was trying to throw up.

Trader was right: *Making Sense of Suicide* doesn't make sense of anything much, including suicide. But yet it told me what I needed to know. Its author didn't tell me. Jennifer told me.

In the margins of her copy of the book, Jennifer had made certain marks—queries, exclamation points, and vertical lines, some straight, some squiggly. She had marked passages of genuine interest, such as might have struck anyone who was new to the field: Like the bigger the city, the higher the rate. Other passages, I can only think, were just being heckled for their banality. Examples: "Many people sadly kill themselves around exam time." "When encountering a depressed person, say something like, 'You seem a bit low,' or, 'Things not going well?'" "In bereavement, make yourself better, not bitter." Yeah, right. Do do that.

It was way after Trader called and I was still sitting up, brain-dead from reading stuff like that—about how unfortunate suicide is, for all concerned. Then I saw the following, marked with a double query by Jennifer's hand. And I felt ignition, like somebody struck a match. I felt it in my armpits.

> As part of the pattern, virtually all known studies reveal that the suicidal person will give warnings and clues as to his, or her, suicidal intentions.

Part of the pattern. Warnings. Clues. Jennifer left *clues*. She was the daughter of a police.

That did matter.

The other end of it came to me this morning as I was clattering through the kitchen cupboards, looking for a pack of Sweet 'N' Low. I found myself dully staring at the bottles of jug liquor that Tobe seeps his way through. And in response I felt my liver shimmer, seeming to excrete something. And I thought: Wait. A body has an inside as well as an outside. Even Jennifer's body. Especially Jennifer's body. Which has consumed so much of our time. This is the body—this is the body that Miriam bore, that Colonel Tom protected, that Trader Faulkner caressed, that Hi Tulkinghorn tended, that Paulie No cut. Christ, don't *I* know this about bodies? Don't I know about alcohol—don't I know about Sweet 'N' Low?

You do something to the body, and the body does something back.

At noon I called the office of the Dean of Admissions at CSU. I gave the name and the year of graduation. I said,

"I'll spell it: T-r-o-u-n-c-e. First name Phyllida. What address do you have?"

"One moment, sir."

"Look, I'm not 'sir,' okay?"

"*I'm* sorry, ma'am. One moment. We have an address in Seattle. And in Vancouver."

"That's it?"

"The Seattle address is more recent. You want that?"

"No. Phyllida's back in town," I said. "Her guardian's surname. Spell it, please."

This information I flipped over to Silvera.

Next I called state cutter Paulie No. I asked him to meet me for a drink this evening, at six. Where? What the hell. In the Decoy Room at the Mallard.

Next I called Colonel Tom. I said I'd be ready to talk. Tonight.

From now on, at least, I won't be asking any more questions. Except those that expect a certain answer. I won't be asking any more questions.

Phyllida Trounce was back in town. Or back in the burbs: Moon Park. She herself had no real weight in all this. And, as I drove across the river and out over Hillside, I could feel a great failure of tolerance in me. I thought: If she wasn't so nuts we could do this on the fucking phone. A failure of tolerance, or just a terrible impatience, now, to get the thing down? The insane live in another country. Canada. But then they come home. And sane people hate crazy people. Jennifer hated crazy people, too. Because Jennifer was sane.

On the phone, Phyllida had tried to give me directions, and she'd gotten lost. But I did not get lost. Moon Park was where I was born. We lived in the crummier end of it—Crackertown. This. Wooden cartons with add-on A-frames or cinderblock shacks with cardboard windows. Now spruced up with pieces of contemporary detritus: The soaked plastic of yard furniture, climbing frames, kiddie pools, and squads of half-dismantled cars with covens of babies crawling around in their guts. I slowed as I passed the old place. We have all moved on, but my fear is still living there, in the crawlspace underneath...

It was over in the Crescent that Phyllida and her stepma now resided. The houses here are larger, older, spookier. One memory. As kids we had to dare each other to do the Crescent on Halloween. I would lead. With a rubber ghoul mask over my face I'd use the knocker, and then, minutes later, a gnarled hand would curl around the door and drop a ten-cent treat bag onto the mat.

There'd been rain, and the house was on a slow drip.

"You and Jennifer, you roomed together at CSU?"

...In a house. With two other girls. A third and fourth girl.

"Then you got sick, didn't you, Phyllida. But you hung on till graduation."

...I hung on.

"Then you guys lost touch."

...We wrote for a time. I'm not one for going out.

"But Jennifer came here to see you, didn't she, Phyllida. In the week before she died."

I'm putting in these dots—but you'd want more than three of them to get the measure of Phyllida's pauses. Like an international phone call ten or fifteen years back, minus the echo, with that lag that made you start repeating the question just as the answer was finally coming through…By now I'm giving myself the cop shrug and thinking: I know exactly why Jennifer killed herself. She set foot in this fucking joint: That's why.

"Yes," said Phyllida. "On the Thursday before she died."

The room was muffled with dust, but cold. Phyllida was sitting in her chair like a lifesize photograph. Like the photograph in Jennifer's apartment. Just the same, only more beat-looking. Straight, thin, weak brown hair, over a gaze that traveled not an inch into the world. Also present was a guy: About thirty, fair, with a balding mustache. He never said a word or even looked in my direction, but attended to the buzz of the earphones he wore. His face gave no indication of the kind of thing he was listening to. It could have been heavy metal. It could have been Teach Yourself French. There was a third person in the house. The stepmother. I never saw this woman, but I heard her. Blundering around in the back room, and groaning, with infinite fatigue, as each new obstacle materialized in her path.

"Jennifer stay long?"

"Ten minutes."

"Phyllida, you're a manic depressive, right?"

I think my eyes came off brutal when I said it. But she nodded and smiled.

"But you have that under control now, don't you, Phyllida."

She nodded and smiled.

Yeah: One pill too many and she slips into a coma. One pill too few and she goes out and buys an airplane. Jesus, the poor bitch, even her teeth are nuts. Her gums are nuts.

"You keep a pill chart, don't you, Phyllida. And a roster. You probably have one of those little yellow boxes with the time compartments and the dosages."

She nodded.

"Do something for me. Go count your pills and tell me how many are missing. The stabilizers. The tegretol or whatever."

While she was gone I listened to the steady buzz of the guy's earphones. The insect drone—the music of psychosis. I listened also to the woman in the other room. She stumbled and groaned, with that unforgettable weariness—that indelible weariness. And I said out loud, "She got it too? Jesus Christ, I'm surrounded." I stood up and moved to the window. Drip, drop, said the rain. It was now that I made myself a promise—a promise that only the few would understand. The stepmother stumbled and groaned, stumbled and groaned.

Phyllida came floating down the passage like a nurse. I moved to the door. She herself had no real weight in this. She was just the connect.

"How many?" I called. "Five? Six?"

"I think six."

And I was gone.

•　　•　　•

Hurry hurry. Because you see: This is where we came in. It's five P.M. on April second. In an hour I meet with Paulie No. I will ask him two questions. He will give me two answers. Then it's a wrap. It's down. And again I wonder: Is it the case? Is it reality, or is it just me? Is it just Mike Hoolihan?

Trader says it's like calling shots in a ballgame. It even fucks with your eyes. You call a good ball out because you wish it out. You wish it out so bad that you *see* it out. You have an agenda—to win, to prevail. And it fucks with your eyes.

When I was working murders it sometimes felt like TV: But the wrong way around. As if some dope had watched a murder mystery (based on a true story?) and was bringing it back for you the wrong way around. As if TV was the master criminal, beaming out gameplans to the somnambulists of the street. You're thinking: This is ketchup. Ketchup from a squeezer that's getting crusty around the spout.

I am taking a good firm knot and reducing it to a mess of loose ends. And why would I see it like that if it wasn't so? It's the last thing I want. This way, I don't win. This way, I don't prevail.

But let's ride with the ketchup—with the procedural ketchup of questions and numbers and expert testimony. Then we can do the *noir.* I may still be provably wrong.

This is where we came in.

•   •   •

On the phone I said that I would be buying, but when we're standing at the bar in the Decoy Room and facing that palisade of booze Paulie No flattens out a twenty and asks me:

What's your poison?

And I say seltzer.

There's a lilt in his voice and his fold-lidded eyes are downward glancing. Since he's apparently twigged that I'm off from CID just now, he seems to think that this is tantamount to a date. Unexpected, because I'd always fingered him for a fruit. Like every other pathologist you ever came across. As if anybody gives a fuck, one way or the other.

We talk about five-irons and RBIs and whether the Pushers have what it takes to beat the Rapists next Saturday, or whatever, and then I say,

Paulie. This conversation never happened, okay?

...*What* conversation?

Thanks, Paulie. Paulie. Remember when you cut the Rockwell girl?

Most definitely. Every day it should be like that.

It beats bursters, right, Paulie?

It beats floaters. Hey. We going to talk dead bodies? Or we going to talk living meat?

No speaks perfect American but he looks like Fu Manchu's nephew. I'm staring at his mustache, which is shiny but also patchy, threadbare. Christ, he's like the guy under the earphones in the Crescent. I mean it's pretty basic, isn't it: Why have a mustache when it just *didn't happen*? His hands are clean, puffy, and gray. Like the hands of some dish-plunging stiff in a diner kitchen. I congratulate myself. I'm flesh and blood, not hide and ice: I can still get the creeps around Paul No, a state cutter who loves his job. But every ten minutes I'm shuddering at the thought of how hardbitten I've gotten.

"The night is young, Paulie. Eric: Another beer for Dr. No."

"... With suicides, know what they used to do?"

"What, Paulie?"

"Dissect the brain looking for special lesions. Suicide lesions. Caused by?"

"Tell me."

"Masturbation."

"That's interesting. This is interesting also. There was a tox report on the Rockwell girl. You didn't see it."

"Why would I?"

"Yeah well the Colonel had it shitcanned."

"Mm-hm. What was it? Marijuana?" Then, horrifically overdoing the mock-horror, he said, *"Cocaine?"*

"Lithium."

Somehow, we all bought the lithium. We all swallowed it. Colonel Tom, down to his last marble. Hi Tulkinghorn, going lean and mean into his own little end-zone. Trader—because he believed her dying words. Because he felt the special weight, as testimony, of dying words. And I, too, bought and swallowed. Because otherwise...

"Lithium?" he said. "No way. Lithium? Fuck no."

Here we are in the Decoy Room, the day after
April Fool's: These, surely, are not Jennifer's jokes. It's
just the world being heavyhanded. Similarly, in
the center of the room, over the white baby grand, the
sleepy-looking...Let me recast that sentence. Over the
white baby grand the pianist with the big hair is playing "Night Train." Of all things. In the Oscar Peterson
style, but with trills and graces. Not passion and mus-
cle. I make my head do a half circle and expect to see,
straddling the next stool along, Arn Debs's tense and
keglike thighs. But all I get are the Monday-night
drinkers, and decoys, decoys, and the wall of hooch,
and the bubbling tideline on No's mustache.

I say so don't tell me. An individual's on that shit
for a time. Maybe a year. What would you see?

He says oh you'd most certainly be seeing signs of
renal damage there. After maybe a month. Most definitely.

I say seeing what signs?

He says distal tubules where the salt was reab-
sorbed. The thyroid, also, would underfunction and
enlarge.

I say and the Rockwell girl?

He says no fucking way. Her organ tree was like a
wall chart. The kidneys? They were dinner. No, man.
She was—she was like Plan A.

"Paulie, this conversation never happened."

"Yeah yeah."

"I believe you're going to keep that promise,
Paulie. I always liked and trusted you."

"You did? I thought you had a thing against slants."

"Me? No," I said. And earnestly. I have no idea what I'm feeling. Random stabs of love and hate. But I gave the cop shrug and said, "No, Paulie. It's just that you seemed so absorbed in your job."

"That's true."

"This has been nice and we'll do it again soon. But just so we understand each other. You keep your mouth shut about Jennifer Rockwell. Or Colonel Tom will put you out. Believe it, Paul. You won't be cutting on Battery and Jefferson. You'll be bucket boy at Final Rest. But I trust you and I know you'll keep your promise to me. That's what you got my respect for."

"Have another one, Mike."

"For the road."

I felt relief like luxury when I added, "Just a seltzer. Yeah, sure, why not?"

Tobe is attending a video-game tournament and will not be home till eleven. It's now nine. At ten I have a phone date with Colonel Tom. So it should work out. I'm sitting here at the kitchen table with my notebook, my tape recorder, my PC. I'm wearing my latest golf pants, with the big gold check, and a white Brooks Brothers shirt. And I'm thinking...Oh, Jennifer, you wicked girl.

It's a phone date with Colonel Tom because I won't be able to do this face to face. For several reasons. One of them being that Colonel Tom always knows when I'm not telling the truth. He'll say, "Meet my eye, Mike"—like a parent. And I wouldn't be able to do that.

Today in the *Times* there's a piece about a recently recognized mental disorder called the Paradise Syndrome. I thought: Look no further. That was what Jennifer had. Turns out it's just this thing where ignorant billionaires—stars of soap and rock and ballpark—succeed in rigging up some worries for themselves. Some boobytraps—pitfalls in paradise. *Zugts afen mir.* Say it about me. I look around the apartment—the hip-high heaps of computer magazines, the dust on my framed commendations. No less than what you'd expect, in the habitat of half a ton of slob and slut. No Paradise Syndrome here. We're clean. In the *Times* there's also a follow-up report and an editorial about the microbes on the rock from Mars. A single smear of three-billion-year-old jizz, and suddenly they're all saying, "We are not alone."

I don't personally believe that her work—her bent, her calling—had much to do with anything, except that it lengthened the band. By which I mean something like: The intellectual gap between Jennifer and LaDonna, Jennifer and DeLeon, Jennifer and the thirteen-year-old girl who murdered a baby over a diaper—that gap feels vast, but might be narrowed by habitual thoughts about the universe. In the same way, Trader was "the kindest lover on the planet"—but how kind is that? Miriam was the sweetest mother—but how sweet is that? And Colonel Tom was the fondest father. And how fond is that? Jennifer was beautiful. But how beautiful? Think about this human face anyway, with its silly ears, its sprout of fur, its nonsensical nostrils, the wetness of the eyes and of the mouth, where white bone grows.

In suicide studies there used to be a rough rule that went: The more violent the means, the louder the snarl at the living. The louder they said, *Look what you made me do.* If you left your body whole, merely mimicking sleep, then this was considered a quieter reproach to those who were left behind. (Left behind? No! They stop. We go on. The *dead* are those who are left behind.)...Still, I never believed that. The woman who cuts her throat with an electric carving knife—you're telling me she's got a thought for anybody else? But yet, three bullets, like the opposite of three cheers. What a judgment. What...highness. What ice. She hurt the living, and that's another reason to hate her. And she didn't even care that everyone would remember her as just another mad bitch. Everyone except me.

•   •   •

Unfair. She was the daughter of a police—her father commanded three thousand sworn. She knew that he would follow her trail. And I believe she knew also that I would play a part in the search. Sure. Who else? If not me, who? Who? Tony Silvera? Oltan O'Boye? Who? As she headed toward death she imprinted a pattern that she thought would solace the living. A pattern: Something often seen before. Jennifer left clues. But the clues were all blinds. Bax Denziger's mangled algorithm? A blind (and a joke, saying something like: Don't grind your ax against the universe. I grind mine against mother earth). The paintings she bought? A blind—an indolent afterthought. The lithium was a blind. Arn Debs was a blind. Man, was he ever. For days I have hated her for Arn Debs. Detested her, despised her. Hated it that she thought I'd swallow Arn Debs—that I'd reckon he'd do, even as a decoy. But then again: Shit, who did she ever see me run with? From the age of eight she watched me hanging on the arms of woman-haters and woman-hitters. Me with my black eye, and Duwain with his. Deniss and myself, holding hands as we limped off to join the line outside Emergency. These guys didn't just slap me around: We had fistfights that lasted half an hour. Jennifer must have thought that black and blue were my favorite colors. What would you expect from Mike Hoolihan—a woman who was gored by her dad? Sure I'd go for big Arn Debs. And why wouldn't I figure, being so fucking dumb, that Jennifer might go for him too? Did she not see intelligence in me? Did she actually not? Did nobody see it? Because if you take intelligence from me, if you take it from my face, then you really don't leave me with very much at all.

You key the mike and you get the squawk that no one wants: *Check suspicious odor.* I have checked suspicious odors. Suspicious? No. This is blazing crime. Fulminant chemistry of death, on the planet of retards. I've seen bodies, dead bodies, in tiled morgues, in cellblocks, in district lockups, in trunks of cars, in project stairwells, in loading-dock doorways, in tractor-trailer turnarounds, in torched rowhouses, in corner carryouts, in cross alleys, in crawlspaces, and I've never seen one that sat with me like the body of Jennifer Rockwell, propped there naked after the act of love and life, saying even this, all this, I leave behind.

A sudden memory. Jesus, where did *that* come from? I once saw Phyllida Trounce. In the old days, I mean. At the Rockwell place. Sweating booze into the blankets, I turned on my side and fumbled with the latch of the window. And there she was, three feet away, staring. In vigil. We looked at each other. No big thing. Two ghosts saying, Hi, mack...

Phyllida Trounce is still walking. Phyllida's stepma is still walking, blundering, groaning. We're all still walking, aren't we? We're still persisting, still keeping on, still sleeping, waking, still crouching on cans, still crouching in cars, still driving, driving, dri-

ving, still taking it, still eating it, still home-improving
and twelve-stepping it, still waiting, still standing in
line, still scrabbling in bags for a handful of keys.

Ever have that childish feeling, with the sun on your
salty face and ice cream melting in your mouth, the
infantile feeling that you want to cancel worldly happiness, turn it down as a false lead? I don't know. That
was the past. And I sometimes think that Jennifer
Rockwell came from the future.

Ten o'clock. I will record and then transcribe.
   I have nothing to tell Colonel Tom except lies:
Jennifer's lies.
   What else can I tell him?
   Sir, your daughter didn't have motives. She just
had standards. High ones. Which we didn't meet.

In the Decoy Room, with Paulie No, when I ordered
the second seltzer—that was a sweet moment. The
moment of deferral. Tasting far sweeter than what I'm
tasting now.

I will record and then transcribe. Oh, Father...
   Colonel Tom? Mike.
   Yeah, Mike. Listen. You're sure you want to do it
this way?

Colonel Tom, what can I tell you. People point themselves at the world. People show a life to the world. Then you look past that and you see it ain't so. One minute it's a clear blue sky. Then you look again and there's thunderheads all around.

Slow this down, Mike. Can we slow this down?

It measures up, Colonel Tom. It all measures up. Your little girl was on a break. No doctor was giving her that stuff she was taking. She was getting it on the street. On the—

Mike, you're talking too loud. I—

On the fucking street, Colonel Tom. For a *year* she was second-guessing her own head. Bax Denziger told me she'd started losing it on the job. And talking about death. About staring at death. And things were coming apart with Trader because she was sizing up some other guy.

Who? What other guy?

Just some *guy*. Met in a bar. Only a flirt thing maybe but you see what it's saying? Don't tell Trader. Don't tell Miriam because she—

Mike. What's happening with you?

It's a pattern. It's all classic, Colonel Tom. It's a dunker, man. It's a piece of shit.

I'm coming over.

I won't be here. Listen, I'm fine. I'm good—really. Wait...That's better. I'm just upset with all this. But now it's made. And you just have to let it be, Colonel Tom. I'm sorry, sir. I'm so sorry.

Mike...

It's *down*.

•   •   •

There—finished. All gone. Now me I'm heading off to Battery and its long string of dives. I want to call Trader Faulkner and say goodbye but the phone's ringing again and the night train's coming and I can hear that dickless sack of shit bending the stairs out of joint and let him see what happens if he tries to stand in my way or just gives me that look or opens his mouth and says so much as *one single word.*